D1713692

info@nabbiesyarns.co.uk

www.nabbiesyarns.co.uk

 twitter.com/NabbieY

58°N

B O O K S

*To my dear wife, Marjorie, and our children ~ Amanda, Sarah,
Jane, Martin, Peter, Simon, and Matthew; and my grandchildren
~ Adam, Holly, Sam, Athene, Max, Madeleine, Kepler, Louis, Millie,
and Catriona; and my great-grandchildren ~ Finn and Alex; and
not forgetting my children-in-law Brian, Guy, Sirichan, Olivia,
Nikki, Tierney, and Dean; and, of course, my grand-dog, Teddy.*

IN AID OF
**GREAT
ORMOND
STREET
HOSPITAL**
CHARITY

*All proceeds from the sale of this book go to
Great Ormond Street Hospital Charity in memory of
my dear son, Simon Macnab Mackenzie,
and my beloved wife, Marjorie Mackenzie.*

A Brief Introduction to my Life

....

I was launched at Craigmore, our house on Shore Street in Ullapool, on the 10th of August 1931 – such a convenient place, just thirty feet from high water.

The event went according to plan, but unlike Mother's three previous launchings I had curls of radiant red hair, rather than raven black, and this was received with great acclaim by Granny, my father's mother, who was herself from the red-headed Macnab clan.

Indeed, so excited was she by this bonny new addition to her clan that she bestowed upon me – as my first name – Macnab.

Agreeing to Granny's demands, without one word of dissent, is something I have never forgiven my parents for.

Oh! She was a determined one.

This name haunted me all through my school years. I dreaded the morning roll call, or having to say my name when a new teacher arrived, and then all my working days after that when I would have to explain that I was not "Mr." Macnab, but rather that Macnab was my Christian name.

It was a torment.

Please – I find myself thinking, even at this late stage of life – let me not have to explain my name yet one more time. I am known now as "Nabbie", and let that be the end of it.

Anyway, name aside, my childhood was a good one living as close to the sea as I did, always with its boats thereon, and it was said with pride that little Nabbie could row before he could walk.

Such exaggeration!

But let me tell you a short tale that goes some way to explain this parental boast.

Before WWII Ullapool was visited by the French cruiser "Gloire". I was excited to see this huge ship lying at anchor when we looked out early one morning. I was five years old then and, rather than going to school, I set off in the rowing boat to get a closer look at this splendid ship – which even had a seaplane mounted on deck.

Getting closer I saw the sailors preparing the plane, and so friendly were they that they were waving at me. Me, in my little boat! I waved back, and that made them wave even more, this had to end – how could I row with all this waving?

End it did, when to my great shock the seaplane hurtled off the deck and seemed to part my curly red hair right down the centre of my head.

Oh, what a fright I got.

I must admit that as I scurried homewards to tell my tale, my rowing was less than perfect - in my panic I clumsily dug the oars into the water, totally forgetting to feather them as one should.

Was this when my life of story-telling began?

I wonder.

A COLLECTION OF WARM, HUMOROUS
& SUSPENSEFUL TALES OF DAYS GONE BY
IN ULLAPOOL, LOCHBROOM AND THE
NORTH-WEST HIGHLANDS OF SCOTLAND

MACNAB MACKENZIE

MAPS

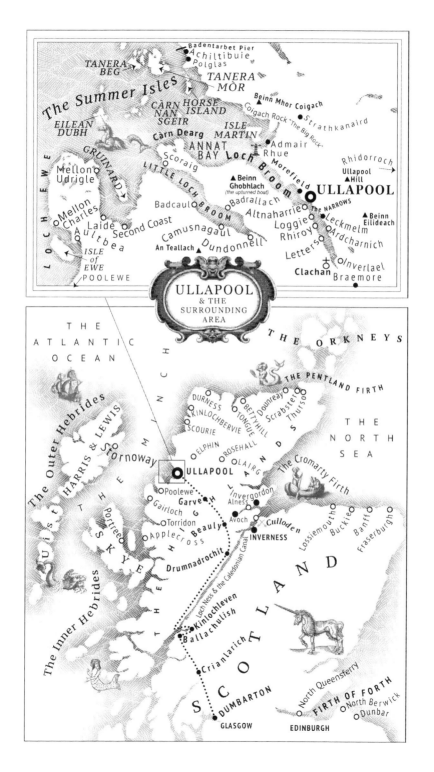

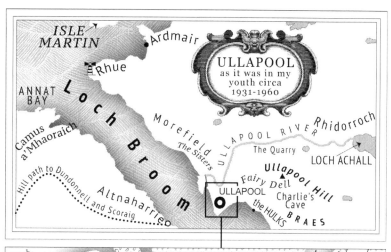

ISLE MARTIN

ULLAPOOL
as it was in my
youth circa
1931–1960

Ardmair

Rhue

ANNAT BAY

Loch Broom

Camus a'Mhaoraich

Hill path to Dundonnell and Scoraig

Altnaharrie

Morefield
The Sisters

ULLAPOOL RIVER

Rhidorroch

The Quarry

LOCH ACHALL

Ullapool Hill

Fairy Dell
Charlie's Cave

ULLAPOOL

the HULKS

BRAES

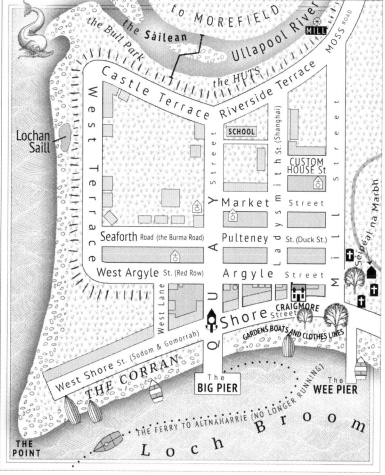

to MOREFIELD

the Sàilean

the Bull Park

Ullapool River

MILL

MOSS ROAD

the HUTS

Castle Terrace

Riverside Terrace

Lochan Saill

West Terrace

SCHOOL

QUAY Street

Ladysmith St. (Shanghai)

MILL Street

Séipeal na Marbh

CUSTOM HOUSE St

Market Street

Pulteney St. (Duck St.)

Seaforth Road (the Burma Road)

West Argyle St. (Red Row)

Argyle Street

West Lane

CRAIGMORE Street

Shore

West Shore St. (Sodom & Gomorrah)

THE CORRAN

GARDENS BOATS AND CLOTHES LINES

The BIG PIER

The WEE PIER

THE POINT

THE FERRY TO ALTNAHARRIE (NO LONGER RUNNING)

Loch Broom

CONTENTS

Lobster Soup 1

An Explosive Issue 7

A Great Skate 11

The Big Beautiful Buick 19

The Travelling Man 27

Jimmy Ferry's Cat 39

The Island 43

The Headmaster and the Bees 69

Chinese Riches 75

A Holy Handshake 79

Arthur and the Seal 87

The Hens, Our Friends 101

What if? 105

The Stone 111

Sausages for Supper 123

Peat, the Great Preserver 129

The Baas 147

The Birdman of Braemore 151

The Egg Poacher 159

Through the Storm 165

The Old Pear Tree 171

Don't Be Long 177

The Refugee 183

The Loss of the Fairweather V 187

The Rainbow 193

A House for the Manager 205

The Black Pearl 209

Baldy and Rover 219

The Forsyth Saga 223

Gold at Braes? 227

Chuckles in Church 237

The Nettle 243

Herring for Christmas 263

Lobster Soup

....

Lobster fishing was and always has been a hazardous occupation. The very nature of the lobster, tending as it does to live among the rocky nooks and crannies along the shoreline, with its oft-times wild and unpredictable waters, makes it so.

Uncle Alec, a stern man of few words, fished for these creatures during the war years. Although a quiet man he was a brave one, having fought in the trenches of Flanders Field in WWI and receiving for his courage the Croix de Guerre. His sometimes crewman, Uilleam MacRae, was younger and rather more easy-going. He too had been a soldier but had been medically discharged from his duties at the very outset of WWII. Although still a little unfit he was of help to the skipper, Alec.

My father, William, was a partner in the little fishing boat they used, a 29 foot Zulu called Daisy, but although he was keenly interested in the sea he had become a tailor, as had Alec, as was their mother's wish. She had no desire to see her sons go to sea.

Now, disregarding this wish, one tailor chose to also fish meaning the other, William, was obliged to stay ashore and look after their shop.

Fishing then was not the mechanised business of today; all the gear had to be hauled by hand and a backbreaking job it was. It was not surprising therefore that Uncle Alec, being Daisy's skipper, was quite pleased when Father volunteered the unpaid services of his strapping son, Johnnie, who at sixteen years old was as strong as a lion.

They were probably rather more hesitant about me as I tended, perhaps, to harbour my strength. Well, I was three years younger.

The day I am about to tell you of was not perfect weather-wise and the creels were set in a rather precarious place below Coigach Rock. With a nasty swell running, Uncle Alec decided that the creels could not be recovered with the Daisy – she being too big and too precious, so it was decided that he and Uilleam should man the small rowing boat to do the task, leaving the Daisy anchored in more sheltered waters, with Johnnie and myself remaining safely aboard.

Off the heroes rowed in the little boat with Uncle Alec leaving us our instructions, something along the lines of – 'Keep the fire going in the fo'c'sle and heat a pan of soup to be ready upon our return from lifting the creels.'

Although we were anchored in sheltered water there was a fearful motion and, what with the Daisy yawing and snatching at the anchor cable, and the rank smell wafting up from the bilges, and the stuffy, oily heat of the dark, cramped fo'c'sle, and to top all that of, the sight of the soup swirling around and around in the big iron pan... well, I felt very green about the gills it must be said.

I retired up on deck to the fresh air where I felt a little better. Johnnie seemed not to mind. Soon though, the waves increased in their intensity, and it was now necessary for him to hold the pan steady to stop it sliding off the stove. Shortly, he too tired of stooping over this hot stove, and he too wanted a spell on deck, so I was ordered back down to administer to the soup and hold the pan firm.

After the cold, fresh air of the deck, the initial warmth of the fo'c'sle was welcome, and I sat there holding onto the pan whilst giving the soup a professional stir from time to time.

My recovery lasted only moments before the queasiness returned with a vengeance. As I was feeling so poorly I was perhaps not quick enough – when the boat rolled sickeningly – to stop the slide of the pan. Off the stove it came spilling half its contents onto the cabin floor.

I yelled out for assistance and Johnnie came scrambling down. Unfortunately, half the soup was on the floor, but even worse – I could not contain the contents of my stomach for one more second, and that too ended up on the floor... along with the soup.

As boys we were rather in awe of Uncle Alec who could be a bit crabbed when things were not going well; therefore Johnnie was a bit worried about the outcome of the accident. I could not have cared less, queasy and dizzy as I was – all I could think of was escaping that claustrophobic, dark and smelly hellhole.

Well, you must give Johnnie full marks for initiative, because when I looked down through the hatch there he was shoveling that which was on the floor back into the pot. The pot he then set back upon the stove and, strange to say, there now seemed to be more soup in it than before. That done he quickly washed and wiped the floor leaving the lino looking shiny and splendid.

Being up on deck, I saw Uncle Alec and Uilleam returning. The small boat was piled high with creels, and both men were in great spirits, heartily congratulating each other on a difficult job well done – now thankfully behind them – and with a good few lobsters to show for it.

They were all smiles, calling out about dinner and wondering if the soup was ready.

I muttered something about Johnnie seeing to it, at which they threw off their oilskins and disappeared down below into the warmth of the cabin.

Johnnie joined me on deck, and we both wondered what would happen next. Although I still felt very green, and Johnnie felt concerned about the quality of the soup, we could not help but giggle.

The gentlemen down below laughed along in their great good humour.

'Ach, they're grand boys, Alec,' says Uilleam, 'That boy Johnnie will go far! Look you, Alec, he even washed the floor while we were at the creels.'

Well, straight off they got stuck into the soup, calling up, 'What grand soup! Come down the two of you – there's plenty!'

I thought we'd die of laughter.

My ribs were sore at my failed struggle to contain the hilarity bubbling up. Down below they could hear us laughing fit to burst, two silly boys, and catching the sheer infectiousness of our mirth, they chuckled merrily in turn as they helped themselves to some more of the delicious soup.

PRINCIPAL CHARACTERS:

Uncle Alec and my father, William, served with the 1/4th Seaforths in Flanders Field in WWI.

ALEC MACKENZIE

Alec rose rapidly in the ranks, and he went through every engagement in which the 1/4th took part. At the battle of Loos on 25th September he had the misfortune to be gassed but made a good recovery. In recognition of his courage, he was honoured with the Distinguished Conduct Medal and the Croix de Guerre from the French Republic.

WILLIAM MACKENZIE

William too was promoted to Sergeant and was wounded on three occasions.

JOHN MACKENZIE

Johnny is my older, and only, brother. He became a Master Mariner and had a long career with BP Tankers, sailing the world over and in so doing justifying Uilleam's prediction.

MACNAB MACKENZIE?

Well, here I am.

An Explosive Issue

....

During WWII Ullapool and District had its very own "Dad's Army" known as The Local Defence Volunteers – L.D.V. Initially, they were armed with anything remotely resembling a weapon of war that fell to hand – a spade, or a fork, or an old broom etc.

Each week drill practice was held at the Drill Hall on Custom House Street. Here the men learned how to handle these weapons of a rather imaginary nature. As time went on the volunteers became known as "The Home Guard" and were issued with proper uniforms and American 300 bore rifles.

Surely they would be able to deal with any landing by invading foreign forces. Fortunately, this did not occur; however, we children found all this new activity exciting, and we even sneaked into the meetings and followed the "Army" when they marched out into the wilds to practice war games.

When our Home Guard was issued with a new machine gun, a practice session was organised for them at the target which was, and still is, up the Rhidorroch Road beyond the quarry. We boys duly followed them there to witness the first firings of this powerful weapon of war.

Oh, how we wished for a chance to fire it, but, naturally, only the Home Guard were allowed.

As instructed, each man in turn lay behind the gun and, as instructed, fired a short burst at the target. All seemed to go well, that was until poor Johnny Calamity's turn came. Even as boys we could see the man was nervous, and as he lay behind the gun with his finger on the trigger we watched intently as he closed his eyes and turned his head away.

Oh, dear, his finger froze on the trigger allowing, not just a short burst of fire, but instead a continuous stream of 303 bullets which hit everything but the target.

Fortunately, Alec MacKay, Hooty's grandfather, had the presence of mind to jump on Johnny Calamity's back and prise his hand off the still-firing gun.

This incident was bad news for us boys as we were no longer allowed to go to the rifle range. Well, we had to admit amongst ourselves that there clearly was an element of risk, but more importantly these oldies had shown that they were not up to it, so a bunch of us founded a unit of our own and, as such, we roamed the hills and glens fighting endless battles.

At a later stage in the war, Marine Commandos from the ill-fated H.M.S. Fidelity came ashore to also use our beautiful landscape for practice. Mortars and other sophisticated weaponry were fired furiously into the hills in preparation for the end game.

You will understand that when the Commandos exercised on our turf the boys' unit was temporarily stood down, but as soon as they had gone our patrols recommenced. Here and there, sticking out of the peaty ground we discovered the fins of many mortar bombs. Cautiously, they were investigated by us youthful boy soldiers but, in our wisdom, we assumed that they were merely practice weapons and so not at all dangerous.

When pulling them out of the boggy peat though, we deemed it advisable to lasso them first with a fishing line and then carefully ease them out while standing well back... just in case.

Becoming confident in the harmlessness of the mortar bombs we decided to lay in a stash of them for future practice sessions. So, gathering up a small arsenal we headed back to the village.

I should have mentioned that the real Home Guard was instructed in its duties by a regular army sergeant, a man of great experience due to his many years of service. He lived in the Drill Hall house, and he found his posting in our quiet village both pleasant and restful. So restful in fact, that frequent visits to the Royal Bar were easily fitted into his daily schedule.

So, here now was the Sergeant marching smartly down Mill Street, past Nona Lang's house where the baby Nona was outside babbling in her pram, blissfully unaware of the drama unfolding just a few yards further on down the brae.

Arriving at the graveyard wall, the eagle eyes of the Sergeant spotted our platoon sauntering into the village, each carrying a couple of mortar bombs.

Seeing the Sergeant we waved cheerily, albeit with some difficulty, our hands being full of bombs.

The Sergeant's normally highly-coloured, whisky-fuelled, red cheeks turned pale. His instinct for self-preservation instantly took over. Flagging muscles steeled, propelling his portly body high over the graveyard, and from the safety of his bunker he then poked up his head and in his best – and loudest – parade ground voice he screamed out:

'Put those bloody things down!'

Before adding, in a rather softer tone, '...*Gently*.'

This coarse language coming from the Sergeant's mouth astonished us, but obeying his orders we nonchalantly chucked the bombs onto the hard road and watched as – after a second or so – the rather bemused soldier slowly rose from among the dead.

The shaken Sergeant then hurriedly resumed his journey, whereupon after downing two quick doubles he phoned the Home Guard and issued an order to come immediately and dispose of the bombs.

A depth of six feet was apparently recommended.

Coming back after lunch we found our mortars gone. We were most upset at the loss of our property and questioned the diggers as to where they were. The men refused to tell, saying it was a state secret: 'War information.'

On reflection, I feel that the bomb disposal squad probably looked for the quickest and the easiest place to bury our munitions. The soft shingle of the shore? Perhaps where the Sailing Club is now?

We shall never know whether or not those bombs were active – and perhaps still are – and, *hopefully*, we never will.

A Great Skate

....

Murdo had two long lines, each line baited with six hundred hooks, and on each of the six hundred hooks a succulent mussel was hanging – all in order to tempt the plentiful haddock feeding on the Isle Martin bank who, for now, were happily swimming and grazing in the depths, totally unaware of Murdo's predatory ambitions.

Hopefully, the weather would be good for a smooth passage from his house at Ullapool Point. Perhaps a gentle breeze from the south would save too much work on the oars, but it so happened that the morn arose with not a breath of wind

No problem, Murdo thought, as he placed the baited lines in the stern of his neat transom-sterned boat. At least the water is smooth.

'So we will just have to row, Jessie,' he muttered amiably to the boat.

You will gather that the lone fisherman had got into the habit of speaking to the boat – his friend and constant companion, Jessie – his beloved 14-foot clinker craft. Indeed, she was more than a friend to him, she enabled him to make a living though, admittedly, not one that would ever make him rich.

So here they were, Jessie floating tranquilly at the water's edge with everything neat and tidy, as Murdo stepped in over the stem and shipped the oars into the rowlocks.

As always he began the trip by making a full clockwise circle to ensure good luck. He would need it! Happily, the pair – man and boat – rounded the point with Murdo instinctively setting his course for the fishing ground, stroking long and regularly, with Jessie chuckling cheerily and thrusting wavelets aside from her sharp stem.

All was well with the world.

As he crossed the mouth of the river though, Murdo felt the chill of a fog drifting in from the open sea. He looked over his shoulder and stopped rowing, spinning the boat around to get a better view of the thickening bank of mist now beginning to draw in around them.

'Damn it all, Jessie,' he exclaimed, 'I don't like the look of this one bit.'

Jessie stopped her chuckling, as though in agreement.

It was decision time for Murdo now, and he pondered hard over all the labour he had exerted.

Perhaps, because of the weather, he might not be able to fish, and then the bait would go bad and be wasted. Should the weather stop him he would have to start from scratch – he thought of all the hours of work he had already put in, never mind cleaning off all the lines he had already baited.

He would have to gather more mussels which was backbreaking work, and then painstakingly he would have to shell each and every one, and again he would have to re-bait all six hundred hooks on the line.

Oh, no, he must proceed despite the fog, did he not have years of experience navigating Loch Broom in all kinds of weather? Looking over at the land beyond the river mouth, he was still able to see – albeit faintly – the outlines of the crofthouses at Morefield. He knew this loch like the back of his hand, and he was confident that he would find the fishing grounds despite the lack of visibility.

He tentatively suggested his plan to Jessie:

'We will hang onto the shoreline there and then make our way seaward. Cautiously of course. And hopefully soon a breeze will come and blow all this muck away, eh, Jessie.'

Jessie sat silently in the water.

In a bit of a sulk, maybe.

On they went, the oars stroking the mirror surface gently. He caught an occasional glimpse of the shore until a denser cloud of mist completely enveloped them and reduced the visibility to zero.

Still, Murdo stroked steadily onward, trusting in his own ability to run a true course, both oars exerting an equal pull. In a silence, broken only by the regular beat of the oars clonking in their rowlocks, the boat glided smoothly on.

Suddenly, to his surprise and consternation, under the boat, he felt and heard a slight scraping noise, and then all forward motion ceased.

'Damn it all, Jessie,' Murdo exclaimed in sheer

exasperation, 'You have run us ashore!'

She did not deign to answer his false accusation.

Murdo pulled in the oars but, on looking around he could see nothing but the whiteness of the mist. He must check that there was no damage to his beloved boat, so making his way forward he peered into the fog-blanketed water ahead. Still he could see nothing, but he knew that he must get out onto the rock and feel around for any damage that may have been done to Jessie's hull. All being well, he could then push her off and proceed on.

Stepping with caution over the gunwale of the boat, Murdo held on to the stem head for balance. The water was not too deep, barely covering, as it did, his rubber-booted feet. He spoke quietly, and with some amount of shame, to Jessie. His accusation, after all, had been false.

'I'm sorry, Jessie, my dear, but I'll soon have us out of this little mess.'

Jessie was angry though, 'Oh! He may say he's sorry, but he still thinks it's all my fault!'

Murdo steadied himself on the hard surface of the rock on which he stood, but because of the poor visibility he could not even see his hands, never mind the ground below him. Squatting down he groped around, feeling the long clean lines of Jessie's hull.

No damage, he thought with relief, but on standing he was astonished to find that the water had risen, it threatened to fill his boots, and Jessie, who a moment ago was hard aground, was now floating free.

Murdo grabbed for a hold of her stem, but his hand slipped, and his beloved Jessie drifted away, leaving him marooned on this rocky island.

He was totally perplexed. How could such a thing

happen? He should have taken a bight of the bow rope ashore with him as he alighted from the boat.

Oh, how stupid am I, he thought, now I am in real trouble.

Once again he stooped down, this time to feel the rock, on which he stood.

Was it a rock?

He knew that he had felt something like this before. His fingers had a memory of such a surface. Somewhere in his long fishing experience, he had indeed felt such a thing.

And it came to him. It's a skate!

In utter panic at the realisation he cried aloud, 'And it's taking me out to sea!'

He was very afraid. At any moment this huge fish could leave the surface to return to the seabed, thirty feet or more below.

But, it did not.

Instead, this huge ray with the scared and shivering fisherman surfing unsteadily on its back, made its way sedately seawards, remaining at a constant depth with Murdo's sea boots making twin bow waves in the calm water.

Ashore, around Loch Broom, residents remarked to each other on this very unusual fog. It had reduced visibility so much so, that most people chose to remain indoors, peering from their fogged out windows. No-one was aware that Murdo, the fisherman, was out there alone and in real trouble.

Alec-Hector the Seer, usually up and about in the early morning what with so many crofting chores to get through, glanced from the little window of his house which was situated at the far end of Morefield.

He had work to do and was impatient to get

started. Looking out over the loch, he thought for a moment that the visibility was improving.

A faint gust of wind was swirling the mist around. Something caught his eye and, focussing on it through some of the wispier strands of mist, he imagined he could see a ghostly form.

'What on earth could that be?' he muttered, 'Surely no-one is out there on such a day?'

He went to fetch his glass, determined to get an answer as to what he had seen.

Horror of horrors! His eyes had not been playing tricks upon him! Wrapped in a swirl of mist he saw what was unmistakably a man, standing on the calm surface of the sea.

He rubbed his eyes and then his glass.

A fisherman it indeed was, leaning to the fore with his oilskin clad arms out to the side, and...

No!...

Motoring along on the surface of the sea?...

In rubber boots?

The mist closed in once more.

Alec-Hector had to sit down.

'Was that truly a man?' he muttered, 'Is the second sight taking possession of me again?'

Despite the poor conditions, he stumbled his way across to the next crofthouse to tell them of the apparition, but finding their door closed and the curtains drawn he realised that the lazy occupants were still abed, taking full advantage of the unworkable weather.

Inside the crofthouse they ignored his cries of alarm, saying, 'Oh, that Alec-Hector, there he is, at it again.'

Unfortunately, not much was known of Murdo's

fishing plans that day, and on the fog lifting Jessie was found, totally intact and undamaged, lying ebbed on the shore not far from where she had started out that morning.

But there was no sign at all of her owner – Murdo. The fisherman had vanished.

Fellow seafarers gathered around trying to envision what had become of the lone fisherman. There were many schools of thought, but chief amongst them was the conclusion that Murdo had stood up to urinate, slipped and fallen overboard.

'Such a thing has happened to many a good man,' they opined sagely.

Even as they talked on, the huge skate was continuing seawards with its reluctant passenger bravely striving to remain upright. Soon, Murdo hoped, the great fish would come in nearer to land and then he could leap ashore, but as he could not swim – a skill lacking in many a fishermen – it would have to be very shallow water indeed to allow this.

At long last, the big fish swung into that bay below Rhue. Murdo seized his chance to escape, and plunging off his precarious perch and through the cold shallow waters, he threw himself, exhausted but thankful, onto the dry land.

His maritime skating trip was finally over.

Our intrepid fisherman immediately started off homeward along the shore. He eventually found himself at Alec-Hector's house, whom he could ask for a moment to dry off and warm up.

Alec-Hector had just heard of Murdo's disappearance and had concluded that his second sight had shown him the soul of the fisherman departing this earthly existence – albeit in a most unusual way.

Poor Murdo, he thought, mortal no more.

The subsequent knock on the door, which on opening revealed "the soul" shivering and wet on the step, promptly blew Alec-Hector's ideas of second sight away. Just as the wind had blown away the mists over Loch Broom itself.

Shocked though he was, he beckoned him into the warmth of his kitchen. But Alec-Hector said not one word to Murdo of the crazy visions he had seen earlier in the day.

You would think Murdo, at least, would be wanting to tell someone of his strange adventure with the skate, would you not?

But no, he was in fact strangely embarrassed by the whole affair. He too refused to speak of it.

No. Not a word about it ever passed his lips, not to Alec-Hector, not to the curious fishermen back in Ullapool, no...not even to Jessie.

And the skate?

Well... who can tell what that creature of the deeps made of it all?

The Big Beautiful Buick

....

In more youthful days, ideas came thick and fast and I, like many others, had my share – I'm thinking now of the purchase of the Buick.

I had wanted to buy a large, spacious car but one that would be cheap to run.

Large? And cheap to run?

'Impossible!' you may say.

But the idea was that the large petrol-powered car would have its greedy, guzzling engine removed to be replaced by a smaller diesel one, of lesser horsepower. Consequently, diesel being very cheap in those days, I would be able to run – economically – this car of my dreams without sacrificing any comfort.

Well, that was the idea.

Where would I get such a car?

Subsequent conversations with my friend, who drove the bus down and back to Inverness, revealed that such a vehicle might be available there due to the owner's retirement from his car hire business. Reputedly, it was very well maintained and would cost the princely sum of sixty pounds as it stood. My idea was coming to life! I could hardly wait to see this dream machine and with the sixty pounds burning a hole in my pocket a meeting was arranged with the owner, Mr. Ross.

Another friend, with a pick-up truck and a tow rope, agreed to take me down there and, if suitable, I would buy the car and we would then tow it back to Ullapool. I could have driven it back, but what with petrol being so expensive... well.

The next day we found our way to Mr. Ross's place of business, and there she was rolled out onto the forecourt from the garage that she occupied every night. Black and beautiful did she look, gleaming in the morning sun. Mr. Ross was carefully going over her immaculate bodywork with a tub of wax polish and a duster.

Love was in the air! An ancient and steady, yet ardent love from Mr. Ross, and an instant rush of love at first sight from me. I tried not to make my feelings too apparent, but after a hasty look over the car, nonchalantly taking a kick at the tyres, as you do when you wish to show casual disinterest, I thrust the bundle of notes into the hesitant hands of this now grief-stricken man.

Mr. Ross understood that I wanted to make off with his beloved Buick, but he insisted that I take a moment to truly appreciate her and so lifted her bonnet, exposing her powerful straight-eight engine. Together we listened intently to her gentle breathing and the sweet purring of her engine.

She was perfect.

I whispered, 'I love you.'

I couldn't help it. The words just popped out.

Mr. Ross glanced at me in surprise, but with warmth, perhaps he was in some way satisfied that this young man was a suitable bridegroom for his soon-to-be-gone beloved.

His sad expression returned soon enough when on helpfully explaining that there was sufficient petrol in her tank to get her to Ullapool, I ungratefully responded – without any feeling for this bereaved gentleman standing there duster and polish in hand – in a callow, almost brutal way:

'Don't worry, mate, we have a tow rope.'

His mournful countenance disappeared in an instant, to be replaced by one of shock and anger.

'Never mind the "Mate", Mr. Mackenzie, I'm telling you here and now that this car has never been towed in all her days, and I'll not see it happening now, do you hear!'

As he uttered each syllable he stabbed his finger into my chest vehemently, glaring with wild eyes into mine. His other hand was fumbling around in his pocket, and for a moment I thought he was trying to retrieve the bundle of notes so that he could throw them back in my face, making the deal null and void.

No, this must not happen! No love story could end so early. I leapt into the driving seat as soon as he released me from his rage and, as the engine was still running, drove quickly out of the yard with my friend in his pickup, totally bemused by the whole affair, following smartly behind.

Of course, looking back, I realise how wrong I was to have referred to Mr. Ross as "Mate".

In his long career driving this sophisticated beauty to functions, both happy and sad, never once had he been addressed so uncouthly. But, callow youth that I was, I put the matter out of my mind instantly and gloried in the possession of such an elegant prize.

Our journey together to Ullapool was indeed pleasant and I enjoyed getting to know my new love. Mind you, it did seem she hesitated slightly each time we passed a filling station as if it were her duty to visit each and every one. I ignored her whims and foot down pressed on, holding the steering wheel firmly, showing her that I was now the boss.

Once home, I subjected my new mistress to an exhaustive and minute inspection, hoping against hope that I would not uncover any radical defects.

Good news – everything was in good order.

The eight great cylinders hummed happily.

The paintwork was bright and gleaming and the coat of arms of her original owner – Lord Tate, of Tate & Lyle no less – embellished her rear doors, quite discreetly, in two-inch gold letters.

Oh, joy!

Father briefly glanced at the lovely car before him without enthusiasm.

'Hmm... Big,' he said. 'Looks powerful.'

These were his only comments. Well, I reasoned, he knew nothing about cars.

I thought about my idea – get a big car; remove the engine; install a diesel one in its place; motor cheaply in comfort. Well, now looking at this fine vehicle I found myself thinking, how could I so vandalise such a lovely creature?

How could I bring myself to throw out such an engine and replace it with a thumping, noisy, smelly diesel? And one with no pulling power? It would have been as though I had pulled my mistress's elegant high heels from her shapely feet only to replace them with a great, hulking pair of wellies.

The idea was sinking in the water.

Let me switch to another matter.

My brother, John, had done well in his career and was now a Master with British Petroleum Tankers, spending much of his time in the Persian Gulf. The family were naturally very proud of him, especially my father, who, had he been given the chance would have been a seaman rather than the tailor he was. John was, in truth, living the life he himself had once dreamt of.

Anyway, Father appeared at our house one morning in a state of some excitement, waving a telegram in his hand, on which were the following words:

Arrive. Inverness. Tomorrow. John.

'We must go to pick him up!' he announced.

'How will we get there?' I asked.

'What's wrong with that car lying at your back door?' he replied impatiently.

'Nothing at all wrong with the car,' I said, 'but it's not licensed for the road at present.'

My normally very law-abiding father looked at me in disbelief.

'Surely a minor thing like a piece of paper on the windscreen is not going to stop you from picking up your brother!' he roared.

I could see that there was no possible answer acceptable to him but for a 'yes' and so agreed that the great vehicle would journey the sixty miles to Inverness on this very important assignment.

The following morning we set off and everything went well. She was made for such journeys, comfortable and fast as she was, and before too long we were in the town.

On approaching the station though, Father, in his extreme impatience to welcome home his son, couldn't wait to get out and opened his door to alight from the still moving car.

'Shut that door!' I shouted as I prepared to manoeuvre her in. I should add that I would not normally have spoken to him thus, but I was quite nervous, and his impatience only added to it.

Anyway, we would park almost on the very platform that John would arrive at – there not being such strict parking restrictions in those days – and there we would wait for the approaching train, bearing our much-travelled son and brother.

Cautiously, and silent as a cat, the great car stealthily glided through the people standing around waiting as the steam locomotive chuffed its way into the Highland capital.

My gaze casually alighted on a group of happy onlookers whereupon I saw, to my horror, among them, chatting in great good humour, a policeman – a sergeant no less – and him totally relaxed with his foot up on a bollard, cheeks glowing, laughing merrily at remarks recounted by his acquaintances.

I must change tack for a moment and talk of family matters, as it pertains to the tale I am telling – well, my mother was a skilled needle-woman and among her many creations were the fore-and-aft caps fondly worn by gamekeepers and the like. One of these adorned my head on this day, and as I sat frozen at the wheel staring at the place where the licence should have been – but was not – I tipped this very hat over my eyes in order to 'hide' from the officer of the law holding court in front of us.

Father was once again wrestling with the door.

I watched anxiously as the police officer changed his stance. Putting both feet back on the ground he slowly bent and stretched before casually turning to view John's train, now shunting slowly alongside the platform. Stiff with concern I watched as the relaxed lawman seem to adopt an entirely different posture. The humorous smiling eyes seemed now to turn to flint; the ruddy cheeks were now granite. Indeed his somewhat tubby body looked to have grown an extra six inches in height, and now, with his massive shoulders thrown back, his presence – to any wrongdoer – was truly menacing.

His piercing gimlet eyes alighted on us. He took in the sight of the beautiful car. Immediately he noted, from the coat of arms on the doors, that this was His Lordship's car, and indeed, there was Lord Tate himself, and him having some difficulty with his door too. He didn't question for a moment as to why the chauffeur had chosen to stay at the wheel.

No.

He knew instinctively what must be done for the sake of goodwill in all ranks, and marching swiftly across he pulled open the door and after standing to attention and saluting smartly, took His Lordship's arm and helped him out.

His Lordship nodded curtly in thanks and rushed off into the thick of the crowd to welcome home his beloved son.

The Sergeant, now having done his great deed for the day, nodded briefly to me – the idle chauffeur –

with some disdain, before marching off to the nearby police station, confident that his little act of kindness might be mentioned in higher circles.

He was, nevertheless, no fool.

He had noticed that His Lordship had no tax disc on display. But... Well, the gentry... An omission probably... He surely would have one.

Soon, Father had John and all his gear loaded back into the big Buick.

John's remark upon seeing my lovely car was cutting in the extreme.

'Where the hell did you pick up this heap, Nabbie?'

I chose not to answer, or indeed point out that if it were not for her and her noble lineage, I may well now be in the police station rather than driving him home. She, after all, was in a league far above us and needed no-one to apologise on her behalf.

With all aboard, we made sail for Ullapool.

The gentle ladylike hum of her beautiful engine belied her gargantuan, monstrous appetite for petrol, and I was reminded once more of her very expensive tastes.

Pushing these thoughts aside I headed home.

'Nice man, that policeman,' said Father, 'and he certainly recognised quality when he saw it!'

'Indeed, Your Lordship.' I replied, looking at him in the mirror.

A sly wink of his eye was all that was needed to tell me that today was the best of days.

The Travelling Man

....

He called himself the "travelling man". It sounded almost posh to his own ears; there was certainly a romantic ring to it, but in reality, he was a poor man, one down on his luck. Others described him as a tramp and treated him as such. What was certain was that this man should not have been out on the road on such a night as this – cold and bleak as it was, with a definite suggestion of snow in the air and miles from any kind of shelter, and he in such a poorly clad condition.

Quite frankly though, he felt that the little village he had left behind had grown tired of his company. This he could understand, having nothing to offer in return for the hospitality he had received from these kind, hardworking people.

Totally broke as he was, he could give no money in return, and not being a hands-on type of fellow

– he never had been – he felt that he would be a liability to them and so did not offer to work for his food and shelter. Nevertheless, he too had talents; unfortunately, they were ones which he could not see much use for in the village, although at an earlier stage in his life these very talents had propelled him to some success in the music halls.

He could make people laugh.

But here in this land, life was serious and there seemed to be little time for laughter.

'Laughter is not an earner here,' he sighed.

Now, with winter close at hand, the travelling man thought to find shelter in a more populous place, where one might expect to find accommodation for one such as himself.

He trudged slowly, and somewhat fearfully, out of the village on what would be a very long walk, to perhaps Dingwall, or even further.

He did not know how long.

Head down, one foot after the other, he just kept on going.

After a time darkness drew in, and looking up ahead through the, by now, steadily falling snow our man could just about make out a little old house by the roadside.

A lonely, isolated house, he thought with a sad smile, much like he himself, and drawing closer he noticed a chink of light from a well-shuttered window.

He was so tired, and cold and hungry too, not having had much to eat that day. He wondered if, by any chance, there might be a "tramp's mark" on the ancient fabric of the house. He had heard of these marks being chalked up on the gate or the doorway by some other man such as he, letting it be known that here one would find a generosity of spirit.

No.

No, as far as he could tell there was not.

But then how could he be sure for he had never actually seen one. He was not a tramp proper, he was just a man down on his luck and these symbols were a language unknown to himself.

The man knew his circumstances were grim, far as he was from shelter, with the miles of road ahead now disappearing into the whiteness of the falling snow and the blackness of the night. His raggedy pockets were empty too, although out here in this lonely place there would have been little use for money – yes, his situation was dire indeed, to say nothing of the rumblings in his empty belly.

Going on would mean a certain death.

Out here all alone.

He would walk, then sit, then die.

He felt ashamed at the realisation that he would now be forced to beg for help in one form or another, but he made up his mind to approach the rather forbidding door, telling himself that pride was for those a little richer than he.

He knocked firmly.

He could hear some movement from within, and at last, the door grudgingly opened, be it ever so slightly, allowing a welcome streak of light to escape into the gloomy night.

A woman called out from within, 'What do you want? Who are you?'

Her hostile voice was far from welcoming, but the travelling man was desperate, and yet not desperate enough to tell her of his true situation. He had a deep sense of pride. Instead he dredged his memory for some sort of *scam* – although scamming her was really very far from being his intention – he racked his brain for anything, in fact, that would sound reasonable and yet might gain him entry to this residence.

Drawing on the skills he had learned in his far-off theatre days, he put on the "style".

'Dear, Madam,' he began, with a gentlemanly bow to the still almost invisible woman beyond the barely opened door, 'I bid you good evening, and the season's greetings.'

The door began to close.

'Madam, Madam!' he cried, trying desperately to smooth the panic out of his voice, 'My name is Joshua McGooligan, and I am a travelling salesperson. I have just left the village having sold much of my stock, and the kind people there suggested that I should call on your good self before leaving the area. And so, dear Madam, here I am, having come all the way here on this fearful night to offer to you my most valuable piece of stock at an all-time bargain price.'

The door creaked back open a little more.

'Should you kindly allow me entrance to your lovely residence I would be pleased to demonstrate this priceless piece.'

At that the door opened, revealing the lady of the house in all her aged country-style beauty. She glared rather balefully at "Joshua", but taking in at a glance that he was not a threat to her person she muttered, 'Well then, what have you got? Where is this great bargain?'

Joshua felt relief, his little story had at least gained him the chance of a moment of warmth in her house, even if it were the briefest of moments.

Mr. McGooligan, as he had now indeed become, swept off his rather battered bowler hat on entering the premises, and holding it between his hands, and bowing ever so slightly once more, he smiled benignly and said, 'Dear Madam, before we get down to business, please honour me with your name.'

"Dear Madam" was starting to thaw out a tiny bit under the onslaught of Joshua's charm.

'And how long have you lived in this charming house – so warm and comfortable as it is?'

'If you must know, Mr. McGooligan,' she said, 'my name is Mary McRobb, and I've lived here, with my now dear departed Charlie, for many a long year.'

The mere mention of her dear Charlie further warmed her towards this strange visitor, as she had no-one to talk of him too.

'Please call me Joshua!' he went on, noting her sadness.

'Och, you might just as well have a seat at the fireside', she said invitingly, 'and show me this bargain piece... Joshua.'

I've cracked it, he thought, but I can do better. I'm warm now, but I'm still hungry, and I must have food. How would he get her to produce something to eat – although on looking around he could not see an abundance?

A prick of conscience?

Well... a little bit.

But he was so hungry.

Aha! He thought as he recalled a story that his grandmother had told him many times as a boy!

And with this in mind, he continued on.

Now that "Madam" was referring to his good-self

as "Joshua", he felt that "Dear Mary", may now be permissible.

'Ahem! Dear Mary...'

How might a bank manager handle this, the actor found himself thinking, before launching in:

'At our age one knows how very expensive it is to live well in the country, what with the price of food, and here – where you live in this fine house – you will have the cost of transport as well.'

All of this was certainly true.

'But with all that said, no doubt your dear husband, Charlie, would have left you well provided for,' he finished with a confident smile.

'I quite agree with you, Joshua,' Mary began, 'living out here *is* very expensive, but I'm afraid to say that Charlie, dear man that he was, spent too much time and money in the village to leave a lot behind.'

Her face grew sad once again as she mulled over her many fond memories of him, 'Oh, Charlie! He was a grand piper you know, in great demand at the weddings and the funerals.'

And then with a sob, she exclaimed, 'Dear, dear, Charlie!'

Soft-hearted Joshua felt his eyes misting over, for truly this travelling man was a soft-hearted man. He felt a stab of shame, but his hunger drove him on.

'Dear Madam, or Mary, should I say,' said Joshua, trying his best to put his own emotional lapse behind him, 'you are going to be glad that I fought my way through that blizzard to get to your door today, as what I have for you is a device which you can use to make the finest soup, and the making of this soup costs you nothing! Imagine! All you have to do is provide a pan full of water and a good warm fire.'

He looked about him, 'I see that you have all that is needed right here, well... except for the main ingredient which – due to your kindness and hospitality – I will give you free of charge.'

Mary McRobb's spirits revived and she demanded that he demonstrate this wonderful invention.

Joshua felt himself begin to warm through, and rising from what had been dear Charlie's favourite chair he busied himself with the demonstration.

Filling the big black pan with water from the tap, he hung it on the chain over the hot fire.

Oh! It was so cosy here now.

He could finally feel his toes again.

The couple conversed amicably together, with Joshua occasionally getting up to stir the warming water with a long wooden spoon.

Finally, in full view of Mary, he delved into an inner pocket and produced a nice flat white... stone!

'This is the fellow, Mary dear, and this shall be your property when I go.'

Into the pot went the magic stone, which would at all times in the future solve any soup problems the lady may have.

From time to time Joshua stood over the pan and stirred the soup, tasting the mixture and describing enthusiastically how it was coming along.

'Oh, Mary, but you are in for a treat. This is splendid... but perhaps a teaspoon of salt?'

Mary excitedly handed him a jar of salt saying, 'Go on then! Put some in!'

'Mmm, even better. You know, Mary, if there was even a bit of turnip or a few carrots, well, that would enhance the flavour tenfold.'

Luckily Mary also had some of these tucked away under the sink, and Joshua briskly gathered them up with a flourish, and into the pot they went. Even the old bone that Mary was keeping for the dog found its way into the magical mix. Joshua constantly dipped the spoon into the soup stirring it around and, lifting it to his mouth from time to time, he would sip and sup as if he were a connoisseur of the finest wines. Mary watched in wonder.

Finally, Joshua declared the soup ready.

Mary was excited.

Joshua was hungry.

The atmosphere in the house was as warm and friendly as it had been in Charlie's days, and Mary happily produced her best china bowls in order to receive this glorious soup.

They sat together at her kitchen table in front of the range, the bowls steamed, the spoons were deployed with abandon, and Mary exclaimed that it was the best soup that she had ever tasted. And all from a stone! What a bargain!

Secretly she was very much hoping that her visitor would not hurry away too quickly, and she wondered to herself if she might offend Joshua if she were to offer him a dram from the bottle of whisky she kept – purely for medicinal purposes, of course – in that cupboard under the stair.

Joshua was not in the least offended, and together they celebrated both the time of the year and the wonderful soup, taking second helpings of the soup – and also of the whisky.

They were genuinely enjoying being together, happy in each other's company – this lonely widow woman and the poor washed-up showman.

He was now so comfortable and at home that he proceeded to sing a few songs remembered from bygone days.

Mary loved music, and memories of the old days were now being stirred from deep within, and she kept repeating, in fond memory of her husband, 'Poor, dear, Charlie. He was grand on the pipes.'

And so they whiled the evening away.

Though the night was wild outdoors, the old couple were surprised to hear voices rising over the wind – children, singing.

Opening the front door to peer out they saw the village children formed into a little choir, their faces bright and their cheeks and noses glowing pink.

They had come from the village that, just that day, he had left.

Their sweet voices sang "In the Bleak Midwinter".

Listening, a tear formed in the eye of the travelling man at the words being sung out to Mary and himself by these innocent children who had never had to live as he did, always outside, always alone.

> 'In the bleak midwinter,
>   Frosty wind made moan,
> Earth stood hard as iron,
>   Water like a stone;
> Snow had fallen,
>   Snow on snow,
> Snow on snow...'

Soon, he thought, he would be back out in that bleak midwinter.

When they had finished their hymn the children piled back into the baker's van for the drive home.

Joshua and Mary stood together at the door waving them goodbye, their emotions a mixture of happiness and grief.

Meanwhile, back in the village, there was a little problem with the preparations for the children's Christmas party.

There was no Father Christmas.

The party committee had been discretely considering the travelling man, who had been in their midst for a long time, for the part. They knew of his history in the theatre and had thought that this talent could be put to good use. Having talked it through amongst themselves they had finally decided that he would be the perfect Santa Claus. But he had disappeared just as they were about to appoint him.

'Where has he gone?' they asked.

The children, on their return, told them that he was at Mary McRobb's house.

The baker was summoned and issued with instructions to return right away to Mary's house and bring back this much-needed man.

Yes, they needed him.

Back at Mary's house things were looking bleak. Mary had said a sad goodbye to Joshua. She had so enjoyed his company, but with the evening at an end, there was no acceptable reason to ask him to stay, she was a widow after all, and so the door had closed behind the travelling man.

Indeed, it had been a wonderful night for both these lonely people, and standing for a moment on the doorstep, snow already covering his old coat, Joshua looked at the dark road with fear and reluctance. It was so dark and so cold out here beyond the warmth of Mary's kitchen, and he had such a long way to go and yet no particular place to be.

In all his life he had never felt so alone.

He stepped out into the night and onto the road.

At that very moment the baker's van skidded to a halt beside him, and the baker – with an envelope in his hand – rushed over to greet him.

'For you!' said the baker, quite out of breath.

Astonished, Joshua opened the envelope to find an invitation to the children's party, but more importantly, it also asked if he would accept the position of Father Christmas.

Yes! He would!

'If,' he stuttered, 'Well... Could Mary McRobb help me, could she be Mother Christmas?'

With a rap on the door, Mary was brought forth.

Would she? Yes, she would.

Indeed, she would have hugged Joshua had that not appeared to be rather forward and unseemly.

And so Father Christmas and Mother Christmas became the very spirit of winter itself.

And the travelling man travelled no more.

And in the warmth of Mary's kitchen, two people sat together, happily supping bowls of Stone Soup on many a cosy evening.

Jimmy Ferry's Cat

....

Picture the scene, dear readers. Those of more mellow years will perhaps remember the location – the house, "Seabank", with its white harled walls aglow above the seashore of Lochbroom, and its eminent walled garden built up from the shore itself, and growing in the grassy garden, a large and leafy rowan tree.

The garden and the house were separated by Shore Street – a quiet road then with hardly a car ever passing, and was lined on the one side by similar houses with similar raised gardens on the other.

Adjoining Seabank to the west was a grocer's shop owned by the family living at Seabank. To the east a lane leading up to Argyle Street. This lane separated Seabank from another house called Craigmore where one of those later mentioned in this story lived.

In short, Seabank and the grocer's shop occupied

the position where the youth hostel now exists.

Jimmy Ferry and family lived at Seabank, and together they ran the shop. The gorgeous animal known as "Jimmy Ferry's Cat" also resided there, to keep the mice out of the sight of the shop's customers.

Of course, dear readers, you will not remember the cat, so let me describe her in all her splendour – she was a beautiful animal, clothed in a mantle of golden, silky, long fur. This cloak was something of which she herself was inordinately proud, and most of her day was spent in the preening and combing of this magnificent fur coat. Stopping on occasion she would acknowledge, with a purr, the complimentary remarks of the admiring passers-by.

'Oh, what a beautiful cat,' they would croon.

On this particular summer's day it was very warm.

Today the cat's best friend, the little boy from next door, found that the wise animal was sheltering from the bright sunshine, under the great rowan tree in the garden. He joined the friendly beast, and together they lay in the shade.

It was perfect peace, not a sound but for the purring of the cat as the boy gently caressed her. It then occurred to the little boy that, because of the unusual warmth of the day, he had had to pull off his jumper, making him wonder if his friend was also feeling too warm.

'Could I do something to help,' he thought, 'Even sheep have their coats taken off in summer time.'

The cat, he reasoned, with her long warm fur, would be much better off without it.

He might be able to help and told the cat so.

'Just stay here,' the boy said enthusiastically, 'I'll be back in a minute.'

He hurried back to Craigmore where he knew he could find the very thing, his mother's dressmaking scissors, long and very sharp as they were. He was pleased, on his return, to find his feline friend was lying just where he had left her.

The cat welcomed him back with renewed and contented purring and lay back ready to enjoy this experience, which was wholly new to herself. She was in heaven as the boy's hands gently stroked her as his sharp shears snipped away at her lovely fur, and before too long her golden tresses had been stripped away.

'Well now, Pussy, that's one side done,' he said approvingly, 'but you will have to lie on your other side now to let me finish the job.'

As we all know cats seldom do what is asked of them and this cat, being no different in that respect, decided instead that it was time for her morning milk and, much to the boy's irritation, she stood up and stalked off towards the house.

'Come back, Pussy,' ordered the boy, 'I have not finished yet.'

Pussy rudely paid no attention.

In the house Jimmy Ferry's sister, Bella, had some of the neighbours in for a cup of tea as Jimmy Ferry's Cat nonchalantly walked in, heading for her saucer of morning milk.

Which of the ladies first saw the lop-sided cat I cannot say, but when Bella screeched and jumped to her feet, thereby spilling her tea down her new dress, there was a general consternation, with the poor distraught Bella wondering what kind of freak accident had overtaken her beloved.

They all rushed out of the house, only to find a

little boy on the doorstep with a big pair of scissors in his tiny right hand, grumbling...

'Pussy would not stay to have the other side done!'

That particular boy's mother thought it was perhaps a good time to leave the party.

This she promptly did, dragging the reluctant lad behind her, as he puzzled over all the fuss when all he had done was help Pussy out of her warm coat.

The Island

....

The Island is the principal jewel in a wondrous setting of smaller colourful gems and from the peak, in the centre, it is possible to view not only the outline of the main island but also the surrounding small islands.

These surrounding islands are inhabited only by birds and seals. No spring rises in the hard, red sandstone and so the lack of fresh water would not permit human habitation for any length of time.

Looking beyond to the west, the Outer Hebrides can be seen on a clear day, lying low on the horizon, a bastion of protection from the wild waters of the Atlantic. To the south and east, the majestic mountains of the mainland rise up. Below these mountains and along the inhospitable shoreline, a scattering of dwellings clings to the soil in unchanging poverty.

But no poverty exists on the Island itself, and the people living here are conscious of the blessings of the place with its plentiful supply of pure, fresh water flowing down from three lochans which never dry up, even in the warmest and driest of summers. Nor, due to the mild climate do they freeze in winter.

The fertile soil, cultivated since the Vikings were here, and perhaps even further back in history if the truth were known, provides good crops and pastures for grazing animals. The principal blessing though is the harbour, providing sheltered waters for fishing boats in even the worst of weather.

There is also, on the more exposed westerly side of the Island, a small Haven in which a boat could take refuge if the need should arise.

Indeed, it is said that this was the first landing place for those early Christian missionaries on their zealous voyage from Ireland to spread the word and who, in their thankfulness at finally stepping ashore after such a long and hazardous passage, erected a stone pillar at the very spot they first set foot.

This is the Halftide Rock, fully exposed at half tide and standing to the height of a man.

THE PEOPLE

Crofting and fishing are the principal occupations, as conditions for both are so favourable that little else is needed from the outside world.

The abundant fish are brought ashore, and processed by the Islanders. The salt necessary for this task is brought in by outside vessels with these same vessels taking away the cured and dried fish and delivering it to far away markets.

The number of people living on the Island does

not vary very much from generation to generation, and as with the coming and going of the fish, nature's interminable tides of birth and death ensure that the elderly and infirm regularly pass away with only a brief disturbance to the placid lifestyle of the people of the Island.

Both fishing boats and crofts are handed down through the generations of the Island's families.

So the eventual death of Dan MacCrimmond raised some concern, as he had no relatives on the Island who could take over his croft, which was one of the best and most desirable on the Island.

It was known that Dan had a nephew, but he had left many years ago, as a child in fact. His father had drowned at the fishing, and he had been taken by his mother to the east coast, to live with her people.

Perhaps the nephew might inherit this fine croft?

Indeed this is what happened; the croft was willed to John MacCrimmond, nephew of Dan.

This news was not particularly well received. It meant that someone, without a great deal of understanding of island life, would be coming among them.

Nevertheless, after Dan's passing, life quickly returned to normal; fishing resumed when the weather permitted, and with their ongoing need for repairs, both inside and out, there was always plenty of work on the crofthouses themselves.

Another constant concern for the Islanders was the continual need to have enough peat to keep their houses warm and dry. In this respect, the Island was, and is, not particularly well endowed. Such peat banks that exist are shallow and poor; however, on the mainland there are plenty and the Islanders organise amongst themselves to sail across, first to cut the peat in the deep banks and then, when the peat has dried out in the wind and sun, to collect it and load it aboard the big skiff to be transported back to the Island. In these necessary tasks, the people help one another without the need for asking, or indeed for any sort of payment.

Such is the way of island life, and only those who have experienced this understand it.

KIRSTY

Recently a new teacher had been appointed to the little island school, Miss Kirsty Campbell, and coming from a rural background herself, the twenty-four-year-old fitted in well with life there. She was young and energetic and full of knowledge gleaned from the bigger world outside, and this she imparted with ease to the eager children in her care, and so Kirsty was highly regarded by all and the children loved her.

Never before had a teacher taken them on rambles as Miss Campbell did, pointing out and naming all the wild birds as she went. She was especially fond of the seals which frolicked among the rocks at the water's edge, and when she called out to them they seemed to understand.

But best of all for the school children, Kirsty took them to bathe in the sea; she even taught some of the older children to swim. She herself was a marvellous swimmer, just like one of the seals that she was so fond of.

Naturally, the young men of the Island looked at Kirsty with fond glances, but she seemed to have no favourites, friends with all – old and young – and always busy with the children, as well as the school where she was the only teacher.

ADIE

It was necessary, from time to time, for the teacher to have the services of a man to do repair work to keep the fabric of the school in good order.

These jobs were carried out by Adie, who was a general handyman on the Island.

Adie was thirty-five years of age, a small, lightly built man with a rather large head and a simple smiling expression. Indeed, he was slightly simple, but he was always willing to carry out the various tasks given to him, not only by the school-teacher but by almost everyone on the Island. Not only was he willing, but he was also quite skilful, and his skills were often required to repair the boats of the Island. In this work Adie excelled, knowing all there was to know about the local boats, even though he himself never went to sea.

He was not a fisherman; he was happy to remain ashore, and since Kirsty's arrival liked nothing better than to be summoned up to the school, or the schoolhouse to do some job or another for her. Indeed he would have done anything for the lovely Kirsty.

Adie himself still lived with his widowed mother in a small thatched cottage just above the pier, and it was from here that the old woman kept a watchful eye on her only son, in the full knowledge that, despite his thirty-five years, he was still but a boy.

Poor Adie, she would find herself thinking.

The eventual arrival of John MacCrimmond to take up his inheritance aroused much curiosity among the inhabitants, with the older ones casting back in their memories to that sad day when they had watched both him and his widowed mother sail away to live with her relatives on the east coast.

What a change the years had brought.

The confused and unhappy scrap of a child that had left was now a splendid figure of a man. They gazed at him leaping lightly ashore where he stood, with obvious military bearing, to survey the scene about him.

Even then it was clear to the onlookers that John MacCrimmond was different, as already he was issuing orders to the crew.

This, of course, was not surprising considering the man had spent many years in military service; still, his pushy conduct did not go down well as the Islanders were not accustomed to following orders, particularly from one as newly arrived as "John the Soldier" – as he came to be called.

Work on the Island was accomplished reasonably efficiently by suggestion and by habit, there were no bosses. The more experienced guided the less so, and then too, they had three Elders should it be necessary to seek advice.

In the days and weeks ahead John the Soldier gradually made his abrasive personality felt, attempting, as he did, to take charge of situations which, in his opinion, were not being dealt with in the most effective way.

The Islanders resented this change and quietly

yearned for the more egalitarian times that had existed before his arrival.

When it came time to bring over the dry peat from the mainland, John the Soldier, as usual, put himself at the centre of the arrangements, urging the use of two skiffs instead of just the one that had normally been used in the past. He was angry when it was pointed out that one of the skiffs was a bit leaky and was awaiting Adie's attention to repair a cracked plank.

'What does it matter if she does leak a bit?' he thundered, 'Surely she can be kept dry by bailing!'

It was pointed out, patiently, that with the boat full of peat it would not be possible to bail the water out.

'Then why has that lazy devil, Adie, not repaired the boat before now?' snarled the soldier bossily, 'We must see to this right away. I'll beach the boat myself on tomorrow's tide, at the pier. Do you hear me, Adie?'

Adie shrugged his narrow shoulders and smiled nervously, but inside he was deeply hurt and resentful too of this bullying tone. He was not accustomed to such behaviour, and over the short amount of time that John the Soldier had been amongst them he had grown to loathe this aggressive man and knew too that most of the Islanders were of a similar opinion except – and this hurt Adie even more deeply – Kirsty the teacher. She seemed to admire him. Indeed, had Adie not seen him going up to the schoolhouse and being invited in by Kirsty herself? He knew that the soldier had spent a long time there because from

49

his vantage point he had watched and waited, in torment, until, hours later, John the Soldier departed after fondly embracing the lovely Kirsty.

True to his word, the following morning John the Soldier beached the big skiff alongside the pier at high water, taking care that the vessel would lean against the stone wall as the tide receded.

When Adie turned up with his tools the boat was drying out nicely, and soon he would be able to crawl underneath to see the damaged plank, but not before he had securely tied the vessel to the pier. It would not do to have the vessel fall over, he told himself, especially if he were working underneath.

The soldier had not seemed to be aware of that possibility, and indeed there he was, already crawling under the bilge with a hoe, scraping off the barnacles in a great show of endeavour. Adie was shocked and concerned for this fellow human being, even though he detested the man.

'You'd better come out of there, John,' whispered Adie uneasily but urgently, 'She might fall on you!'

'Don't tell me what to do, you little runt!' snarled the soldier, ignoring his words and continuing to scrape away angrily at the barnacles, 'Get in there and fix that plank!'

Adie, shocked at the cruelty of his tone, climbed up on to the pier with the intention of securing the skiff. He could clearly see that it had not nearly enough list. Now dangerously upright it could topple at any moment – alas, a black fury had started boiling in his mind, and as it grew it filled his head with a roiling rage to the exclusion of everything else and so, instead of securing the boat as he should have, he sat calmly down on the edge of the pier.

He could hear the soldier scuffling about under the bilge with the hoe, and he could see the boat trembling in her precarious state of balance.

Adie put his feet on the gunwale of the skiff and gently pushed. The boat moved from the wall, hanging for a second in perfect equilibrium, then crashed down on the man underneath. He heard the noise of the soldier's last breath being driven out of his crushed lungs and the snapping of his ribs as the bilge keel ground him into the pebbles of the shore.

Realising with horror and panic the result of his act, Adie jumped down to the shore and, crying out for help, he made futile attempts to lift the heavy boat off the trapped man. Five strong men would have been required to lift the skiff of the soldier, far less poor Adie, the weakling.

It was not Adie's cries for help that brought his mother scurrying to the scene.

No.

The old woman had been watching out of the doorway of the cottage in her usual anxiety for her son, and seeing the train of events unfolding she had run to the shore to stop Adie, but too late.

One look told the horrified mother that the soldier was beyond help. With a heavy heart she ordered the panic-stricken Adie to run at once to the nearby houses to get help, but in her devotion to her beloved child, she told him to say – only – that the skiff had fallen over on top of poor John.

Adie ran, urgently summoning the men with his desperate cries, and soon sufficient power was gathered to heave the heavy skiff upright and so release the crushed corpse of John MacCrimmond.

Afterwards, Adie had little to say, except that he

had, in fact, warned John the Soldier about going under the boat without securing her to the pier, and that a breeze of wind had got up and had blown her over before he had time to put a rope on her.

This then was Adie's story, told just as his own mother had told it to him.

AFTER THE ACCIDENT

The community was shocked at the sudden death of John the Soldier – a man in the prime of life and so splendidly handsome. But truth to tell, among the working folk of the Island there was a subtle sense of relief. Sorrow, yes, at the dramatic nature of his passing, but a sorrow that faded away in quick time as life resumed its comfortable old pattern.

Kirsty was, of course, devastated at the loss of her lover. She found, in the days and weeks ahead, great difficulty in concentrating on her work at the school and was often to be seen wandering alone on the Island. Brooding and grieving over her loss, she found some slight comfort in sitting near the seals which came ashore to lie in the sun on the flat rocks.

Adie too was a changed man. Oppressed by the heavy burden of his guilty secret he was, for the first time in his life, reluctant to get on with the tasks he had performed so well in the past.

DRINK

As you may expect, there was strong drink on the Island. In a secret place, they had their built own still in order to provide a certain amount of lubrication for the regular ceilidhs. Also hidden away was a cache of gin, given to the Islanders by the crews of the Dutch boats that came from time to time, leaving behind them a bottle or two in return for the kind hospitality that they had received.

Oh, it was all very controlled and drunkenness was rare, but Adie, for the first time to anyone's knowledge, began to take a drop too much. His work had become irrelevant to him, and he avoided going to the school to do jobs for Kirsty.

Kirsty, in her grief, understood his falling to drink. She had a big heart and there was also room in it to grieve for Adie, for whom she had a great fondness.

'Poor, Adie!' she thought, 'What a shock it must have been for him.'

When the fresh water pipe from the well choked up with silt, Kirsty, who had not seen Adie for many days, was forced to send one of the boys for him so that he would come and sort the problem.

When he turned up, hours later, she was disappointed to see that he was the worse for drink.

'Oh, Adie!' she exclaimed sadly, 'What in the world is happening to you?'

She sat him down and took his hands in hers, saying, 'You've never been the same since the accident. You were never one for the drink. I know you got a fearful shock – as we all did – but we will have to try and get over it!'

Adie looked into Kirsty's bright, kind eyes with his own – red and drunken and bleary as they were – and before he knew what he was saying he blurted out all the hurt held tightly within, telling her of the hate he had had for the departed soldier.

'I'm glad the brute is dead!... And the Island is a better place for it!'

Kirsty was paralysed with shock.

'I did it for the sake of the Island, and everyone

is pleased! He was no good, and you are better off without him. He was nothing but a bully!'

With these words, Adie stumbled out of the school.

Kirsty was still and pale. Was this the drink talking, she wondered, or was there something in his boasting words. Could the gentle Adie have something to do with John's death? After much worrying, Kirsty determined to report the matter to the Elders of the Island. They would know how to resolve this awful problem.

ISLAND LAW

Of course, the Island was, and is, part of the Kingdom. Technically it was subject to the laws of the country, but in this place, so remote and trouble-free, the Islanders had their own system for keeping order and chose not to rely on the mainland powers. Island law had existed virtually unchanged for countless generations and to administer the system the Islanders elected three Elders.

At this time the senior Elder was Archie Macleod, and to assist him – if indeed that was ever necessary – he had the more youthful Hamish MacRae and Dugald MacLean. It was therefore to Archie Macleod that Kirsty went with her worries.

Archie, sitting to one side of the fire in the warm kitchen, listened patiently as Kirsty told of her worries about Adie's "confession" and said at last:

'Well, Kirsty, I hope that what we have here might be just poor Adie's ravings. With him being there at that dreadful scene, well... he must have got an awful fright, but it is worrying that he's taken to the drink.'

'However,' he added, 'this matter must be dealt with. Justice must be done.'

Archie thought for a few minutes before adding, 'I'll have a word with Hamish and Dugald today, and they will go over to Adie's and bring him before me for questioning this very night and, as a complainant, Kirsty, you must appear here too.'

She was surprised at the speed of action but grateful that her story was being taken seriously, and agreed to attend the hearing.

When evening had fallen, Kirsty, deep in thought, made her way towards Archie's house. Although she was not fully aware of the island's customs yet, she did know that under the law of this place only the Elders were responsible for enquiring into and carrying out its demands. It was therefore not necessary to have others, who were not involved, at the hearing. Consequently, most of the islanders were unaware of the events unfolding that very evening.

The arrival of Hamish and Dugald at the poor dwelling shared by Adie and his mother went unobserved by all. Their knocking brought the old woman to the door, and she knew in her heart, of course, why they had come. Having taken the heavy burden of their guilty secret onto her poor old shoulders she knew there was little more she could do to influence events.

Hamish, attempting to calm the poor agitated woman standing there wringing her gnarled hands together, merely said, 'Archie would like Adie to come up and have a word with him.'

The old woman called weakly over her shoulder to the small figure crouching over the glowing embers of the peat fire in the dimness of the cottage.

'Adie, you're wanted at Archie's. You'd better go at once and see what he has to say.'

Not having been on the bottle since the previous day he was quite sober, and in his usual gentle way, he did his Mother's bidding without question, going willingly with Hamish and Dugald.

The three made their way up the hill leaving the old woman alone and weeping. The deeply etched lines on her kind, old face were like ravines, eroded away through the many years and the many tears she had cried over the cares and worries she suffered for her dear son.

THE HEARING

This was not a courtroom with lawyers in wigs and pomp and ceremony; no, it was just a small group of honest Island folk searching for the truth.

When that was established appropriate measures would be taken, under Island Law, to mete out justice. Archie Macleod, sitting at the head of the well-scrubbed table, began by thanking all for coming, and stating that he hoped that the meeting would clear the air regarding thc unfortunate death of John MacCrimmond.

Adie, sitting at the foot of the table, reminded himself that all he had to say was what his mother had told him, and he felt confident that his story would be accepted.

The Elders seemed friendly towards him and, as Islanders themselves understood the correct procedures for beaching and working on boats.

But, Kirsty, whose eyes had been so gentle and loving in the past, stared intently and with some hostility into the face of Adie, as he sat next to Archie.

Indeed, she thought back to the outrageous remarks uttered by this man.

Adie, with guilt filling his heart, could not look Kirsty in the eye.

Beginning the questioning, Archie, in a quiet voice, said, 'Adie, think back now and tell us, truthfully, exactly what happened that day.'

With some confidence Adie trotted out the version of events as suggested by his mother and, by the look of it, at least amongst the men, his story seemed to gain acceptance. Both Dugald and Hamish spoke in support of it, knowing of John MacCrimmond's ignorance with regard to nautical matters.

Who in their right senses would work under an unsecured boat?

How careless.

Was this not, in fact, what they all thought?

Then Archie turned to Kirsty.

'Now, Kirsty,' he said, 'I would like you – with Adie present – to repeat what you told me this morning.'

Kirsty looked into the face of Adie with such a level of intensity in her gaze, that although he wanted to meet her eyes, which was also her intent, he could not – he was indeed forced to cast them down.

She spoke with such sincerity and vehemence that she commanded the full attention of those present.

At the completion of her statement, Adie's face crumpled, and he cried out, 'It's true... I pushed the skiff over on him, I hated him so!'

The room fell silent, a silence broken only by the sound of Adie weeping. At last Archie spoke, thanking Kirsty for her help in this tragic matter and saying that whatever action was to be taken now would not require her presence, and so, consequently, she was free to leave.

This Kirsty did, making her way homeward over

the dark island and wondering sadly what would now happen to that poor creature.

'Poor, Adie!' she said to herself.

But then the thought of her lover made her cry out, 'Poor John...!'

And her heart hardened.

THE VERDICT

With Kirsty gone the proceeding recommenced with Adie now flanked by the junior Elders.

Archie, his face grave and ashen, spoke out:

'We have all heard the confession of Adie to the wilful murder of John MacCrimmond. So I ask, do you Hamish and Dugald, as Elders say guilty or not guilty?'

With some reluctance, the men muttered, 'Guilty.'

Archie spoke on, 'Adie, you have been found guilty, and as the law of this Island demands, I do sentence you to suffer at the ancient Halftide Rock. You will be made fast to the rock allowing the flood tide to cover you, as it will, and thus we surrender you to the power of the sea which will itself determine your future. Upon the ebb, you will be released and returned to the community in the condition you are found. Have you anything to say, Adie?'

The condemned man shook his head, and Archie announced that the sentence would be carried out the next day after the people of the Island had been informed.

Word of the Elders' decision, with regard to John the Soldier's demise, was received with disbelief and then with shock that the sentence was to be carried out so quickly. But then this was the Law, the unspoken law that they all abided by, and to delay its implementation would only cause more suffering to Adie, and to his poor mother – herself near the end of her days.

The following morning it was as if the Island had been deserted. Nobody ventured outside. The doors were hard closed and the windows shuttered and blind. It seemed as though death itself stalked the land. The only movements were those of the Elders preparing the light skiff for the piteous passage which the doomed man, at the appointed hour, would take to serve his sentence.

So that the condemned man could be secured to the pillar of rock, the Elders would have to be there three hours before high water. This they arranged, allowing sufficient time to row the skiff the relatively short way from the harbour to the seaward Haven – the location of Halftide Rock.

In a confused state and seemingly unaware of what was happening, Adie made no difficulty on being taken from the locked byre at Archie's croft and then to the pier. Even as he stumbled past his mother's house, with its windows tight-closed, he did not lift his eyes from the ground.

But he must surely have heard the anguished moans emanating from within their little crofthouse home.

No-one watched the skiff leave.

Its four oars pulled strongly away from the shore with Dugald and Hamish rowing, and Archie and the forlorn figure of Adie sitting together in the stern.

Upon reaching the Haven Adie made no attempt to escape, indeed, on stepping out of the skiff he even helped to pull the craft ashore. He remembered this place, having come to it overland on several occasions, but never by sea. There was the stone pillar standing tall at the half tide mark, now fully exposed, high and dry. To this ancient memorial stone Adie was led, dazed and unhappy, but brightening for a moment when Archie allowed him a slug of whisky from the bottle he had brought from the boat.

Then with rope, the boy, with not one word of protest, was bound tight to the pillar by the Elders with an expertise that is second nature to fishermen.

Now that Adie was securely bound to the stone, Archie MacLeod made the final address.

'Adie, you have been found guilty of causing the death of a fellow human being, namely John MacCrimmond. We, the Elders of the Island, leave you to the nature of the sea to do what it will with you, and in the time left to you may you reflect upon your wicked deed.'

Once more Archie put the bottle to Adie's lips, letting the raw spirit gurgle down the wretched creature's throat.

With that, the Elders walked back over the rocky foreshore to the skiff which was now fully afloat on the rising tide.

'Oh, Adie!' they muttered to themselves. He was, after all, one of their own, like a son and brother to them – and they were filled with anguish.

With a last glance back at the bound man, they bent to the oars and rowed back to the village.

The old woman stirred from her couch.

Hours had passed, and the chinks of light which had been streaming in from outside could not now be seen. She realised, with guilt, that she must have slept for an hour or two.

How was that possible?

And with her son out there.

Oh! Her precious son!

She remembered, in her long life here on the Island, only one occasion when that dread and cruel punishment had been meted out. The outcome then was what certainly would occur on this occasion.

There could be only one outcome!

She abandoned herself to her despair.

It was not permitted for any living soul to witness this punishment but, still, the old woman wished to be with him. She had been there at his beginning and she would be there to comfort him at his end.

Her dear son, her dear boy, Adie.

As the evening closed in she hastily followed the steep and rocky path towards the Halftide Rock.

For the tide waits for no man.

ADIE

Adie may have been thought simple by the islanders – and the spirits he had drunk had certainly added to his general confusion – but even with all that, he well knew that when the tide was full the water would be well over his head. He was, after all, a small man, considerably smaller than the stone pillar to which he was bound, the top of which would soon disappear under the tide.

Although bitterly regretting his actions and that mad impulse which had brought him to this place, he still held hatred in his heart for John the Soldier.

Filled with self-pity his thoughts turned to his mother and, as he felt the icy chill of the rising water spilling over the tops of his boots, he was filled with an awful fear, and he wished desperately that she could be here with him now.

In his anguish, he cried out into the silence.

A sad screech echoed back to him.

He strained to listen.

A seed of hope grew in him, as slowly and relentlessly the water rose in the calm Haven.

Another call cut sharply through the dusk, and then he heard a powerful beating of wings and the silvery ghost of a heron, itself retreating from the advancing tide, flew over.

His spirits sank.

And yet?

From afar he could hear a call sweeping in with the wind. It wrapped itself around him – a voice, so familiar, grew in the approaching night.

'Adie...! Adie it's me!'

Oh, Mother!... Mother! I am so sorry, Mother,' he cried.

She waded out into the deep black water.

An icy chill seeped into her ancient bones but she felt nothing, only a longing to be with her boy.

Desperately she hoped that she might untie her son and, though it would be a grave sin against the Law, she tore at the binding ropes.

But her old hands were weak and the ropes hard.

The knots were like stones.

It's useless, she thought.

Undoubtedly the sea would soon cover her son and the retreating tide, denying him his need for a breath of air, would take with it his very life itself.

The old woman, while comforting her son, both now waist deep in the cold sea, allowed her mind for a brief but golden moment, to wander back to her childhood days when she had played with the other children of the Island at this very place.

Oh! The fun they had had.

She found herself smiling at those innocent and distant times.

She thought of the sticky burrs they had thrown at one another and the hollow tubes of the old burr bushes that they had blown bubbles through.

An ember ignited in the old woman's mind.

She said to her son, 'Adie I am going to leave you now, but I will be back in just a while!'

'Yes, Mama. I'll be all right. You just go on home.'

Finding a new strength, and immune to the cold and the waves, the old woman waded back through the rising water to where the burr bushes grew, and she quickly snapped off a stem. The stem had weathered so much that the pithy centre had dried out and was gone, leaving a perfect tube.

With this, she hurried back to the water's edge and her son.

'Adie, my child,' she said urgently, 'Listen to me. There's a chance for you. Do exactly what I tell you. I'm going to put this reed in your mouth and when the tide rises lift up your face and breathe through it until the water ebbs away. You must be careful and not let it drop because I will not be here to help you put it back.'

Her voice was filled with love and encouragement,

'I know you can do this Adie, and when they come for you... say nothing about this.'

Adie had difficulty imagining how this would work, but if his mother said it would, well, it would. A wave of confidence swept through him.

He held the tube in his mouth.

He could breathe.

It was now time for the old woman to hurry back home. She herself was fearful of the outcome, but hiding her fears, and instead smiling into his eyes, she bade him farewell, and struggled, in her heavy waterlogged clothes, through the water – now chest height – back to the shore, hoping against hope that her son could carry out her instructions.

Looking seaward it was now too dark to see him and, in anguish, she began the long hard trek over the hill to her cottage on the other side.

At the appointed time, with the full moon bright in the sky, the Elders launched the rowing skiff and set off once again to the Haven. Knowing the inevitable outcome of the sentence, they had taken with them a canvas shroud in which they might carry Adie back in a fitting and decent manner.

On rounding the rocks at the entrance to the Haven with the brightness of the moon to aid them, it was possible to see, even at a distance, the body of Adie still rigidly secured to the pillar of rock, his head slumped on his chest.

They saw the high water mark, still wet, high above his head on the stone pillar. In sadness they walked towards him, holding the shroud.

Adie, blue and chilled to the core, awoke with a start on hearing them approach, and the Elders, on seeing his corpse-like face rise up to greet them, looked at one another in dread. The icy blue veil of death and the ghastly grimace of the drowned man lifted away.

Here was Adie – alive!

How could it be?

His familiar smile lit up his cold, glassy face, and he said, 'Well, boys, that wasn't too bad after all!'

The Elders shook their heads in disbelief and hurriedly cut the ropes, freeing the man whom the sea itself had spared. Hardly a word was spoken on the passage back to the harbour and the village and, on landing, the Elders accompanied Adie back to his mother's house above the pier.

Well, they thought, it was the least they could do for the poor soul, wet through as he was from his long immersion.

Sadly, it was then that Adie's mother was found, laying there on her couch, quite dead. The exertions of her recent actions had proved too much for her poor, worn-out body. There she lay, at peace now, her ancient wrinkles smoothed out in death and with a curious smile upon her countenance.

There is no doubt that the Island people were pleased, if a little puzzled, to see the gentle and useful Adie, back in the land of the living.

Kirsty could scarcely believe it. How could he survive underwater for that length of time? Even a seal could not do that, and Adie was certainly no seal. He could not even swim. So even she, an educated and clever woman, fell to superstitious thoughts.

Once more, the Island returned to its old ways, and Adie, having been judged and duly released by the sea, and subsequently believing that he must be totally innocent of any wrongdoing, took up his jobs again with enthusiasm, even repairing the big skiff which had 'fallen over' at the pier. It had required the replacement of many fastenings – the body of John the Soldier not having provided a sufficient cushion to prevent her getting badly shaken up in her fall.

Kirsty still felt uneasy at having Adie at the school, but he did seem to be behaving himself with regard to the drink, and he carried out his various tasks efficiently. She worried though, that he seemed to wish to hang about long after he had finished, and she felt that, with John now gone Adie would be pleased to take his place. The very thought of this made her shiver, and she had a terrible feeling that justice had not been done, that the sea had, somehow, been tricked.

She still went to sit amongst the seals, and sometimes in the evening, as darkness fell, she had the urge to swim at that remote place in the company of the friendly animals.

On one sunny day Adie, now without the governing influence of his mother, followed Kirsty. Hiding away he watched her as she spoke to the animals, and then he saw her strip off her clothes and join the seals with an expert dive from the rocks.

Not able to contain himself he rushed to the water's edge, calling out to her.

Kirsty was shocked, she had thought herself to be alone, but her shock soon turned into cold anger. She now knew that she had a real problem with this man – and to think that it was more than likely that he had been responsible for her John's death!

Indeed, she was now certain of it.

Adie had wanted her all along.

His voice was still calling out to her, 'I wish I could swim, Kirsty. We could then swim together!'

Suppressing her anger, Kirsty called back to him, 'Indeed, Adie, anyone can swim. You should try it, come on in.'

And with that she swam, with nary a ripple, to join the seals which had now moved out to deeper water, away from the frightening presence of the man.

'Anyone can swim!' muttered Adie, 'I can swim!'

He began to remove his boots and then his outer clothes, and standing somewhat fearfully for a moment on the rock, his drawers dangling, he nervously prepared himself.

He thought back to the Halftide Rock and smiled at his fears – had he not indeed conquered the sea?

And anyway, Kirsty, smiling over at him as she was, was she not there to help if needs be?

Reasoning thus he plunged from the rocks into the water with an ungainly splash.

The frantic efforts of the drowning man should perhaps have alerted Kirsty to his plight.

But, strangely, she seemed not to notice Adie floundering around and instead, swimming smoothly and calmly further out and away, she headed towards the seals in their deep, dark water.

Returning a little later, only slightly fatigued, Kirsty felt refreshed and powerful.

Taking her time and enjoying the feeling of the water evaporating off her skin in the warm last rays of the evening sun, she dressed and returned to the schoolhouse, without even noticing the untidy heap of clothes and the empty boots above the rocks.

How well she felt, she thought to herself, indeed so much better now than at any time since John's death, and in that moment within her body, she felt the first fluttering, watery movements of the next John MacCrimmond.

The Headmaster and the Bees

....

At school the cooks were angry. Although there were plenty of potatoes in the school garden, they were still in hiding underground. Whoever was responsible for digging them out of their warm earthy bed and delivering them to the kitchen had neglected to do so.

The principal cook complained to the Headmaster who took on their anger in turn, muttering, 'I'll see to it!' before heading towards a certain classroom, where he knew that he would find a couple of boys who would no doubt be wasting their time.

He did indeed find two such boys, and they were promptly sent out with instructions to proceed without delay to the aforementioned garden and dig up sufficient Kerr's Pinks from the abundant crop to fill the basket supplied.

The boys were, at first, quite pleased with their little job – it was a grand morning after all.

In no time the basket was full, however, there was a reluctance now, with the day being so softly sunny and warm, to return to the classroom – after all, nobody had mentioned that the potatoes were immediately required. Instead they relaxed in the sunshine watching the bees busily coming and going from their hive to the garden, listening to the drones of contentment as each wee bee went about his work.

So much better than listening to their teacher.

Boredom soon set in, as is the way with boys, and, as there were lots of little stones lying around they began a game of "who-can-hit-that-dish-of-water-in-front-of-the-hive". Coming from homes just above the beach, where there are millions upon millions of perfect throwing stones, the boys were very good at the game. In the school garden though, the stones lacked the projectile perfection of those at the shore, thus it was not surprising that they had a few misses.

Indeed a few overshot and hit the Bees' home. Murmurs of discontent were now to be heard emanating from the dark interior of the hive.

Imagine the discord within the community.

The Queen screaming out over the intercom, 'We're under attack!' and hence issuing orders for her brave troops to venture smartly forth, fully armed and ready to do battle with whomsoever was guilty of this outrage.

And so, furiously answering their queen's call, the bees, armed with the latest sting weaponry, surge out of their hive and on seeing two indolent-looking boys lying back enjoying the sun think:

'Not them, surely!'

But then though their wee bee eyes they spot a fat little human rushing out from the school.

That's the one.

He was obviously intent on resuming his attack.

The bees could tell he was mad with rage.

He must be dealt with.

The leading bee, on giving the appropriate buzz, takes his troops into battle and the whole squadron home in on the irate, but wholly innocent, Headmaster.

The two boys quickly clamber to their feet and picking up the basket of spuds wisely saunter to a safe position, keen to watch the scene unfolding before them.

Perhaps the Headmaster has a fear of bees; anyway today he has reason for it, and seeing and hearing the dark swarm angrily heading for him he panics, running blindly at top speed towards "Shanghai", or Ladysmith Street as it is more properly known.

Here there is a wire fence to be got over and the bees are already upon him, jabbing ruthlessly anywhere they can find purchase.

The wee man powers on, knowing that he will need all his speed – and agility too – in order to hurdle over the spiky fence, damaged as it is through the illicit taking of shortcuts by one and all.

Accelerating towards the fence, the Headmaster springs into the hurdling configuration he had last used many, many years past, although on seeing him running now it is hard to see the athletic youth he had once been.

He leaps.

Right leg arching forward, left leg cocked back.

The boys watch with great appreciation as those dangerous rogue wires atop the fence reach out and grab the loose crotch cloth of the Headmaster's smart tweed trousers.

A ripping is heard.

Thinking it is an escape of wind – the kind of thing always guaranteed to make a boy giggle – they burst out laughing.

Oh, but it was worse – or maybe better? – thought the boys on seeing the large piece of loincloth now fluttering like a flag on the fence.

Having cleared the fence, well almost, the athletic Headmaster – to the astonishment of the housewives out doing their morning chores – rushes headlong down Ladysmith Street.

The village ladies called to one another excitedly:

'Did you see yon?'

The Headmaster, whom they all very much admire, being the man responsible for hardening up their children – through his regular lashings of the belt – freely given in preparation for the hardness of life after school, was running away, like a baby – from a few wee bees.

Slowing down to catch his breath and to ease the painful stitch in his side, he now felt a distinctly cold draught below and hastened home to Market Street, whereupon, after a meticulous testicular inspection and finding everything to be in good order, he carefully donned his Sunday trousers.

Now suitably attired, the Headmaster, knowing the importance of resuming his command, made a speedy return to his school. It would not do to appear to be a Captain deserting his ship, leaving his crew and passengers to the mercy of the Bees.

He need not have worried.

On his return, he found perfect peace aboard.

The boys were back in class.

The cooks were happy.

And a good meal had been prepared.

Whilst reflecting upon the bothersome nature of both Boys and Bees, the Headmaster at last felt at peace.

The war was over... for now.

Chinese Riches

....

History. I can picture the scene in my mind – the great gatherings of the merchant ships of Great Britain, heavily loaded and lying peacefully at anchor in the temporary security of Loch Ewe, awaiting suitable weather and war conditions to sail under Admiralty orders to Murmansk.

During their arduous and dangerous voyage, they would be at continual risk of attack from both air and sea and so they were to be shepherded by the fighting ships of the Royal Navy.

As a boy, I did not see these ships at anchor in Loch Ewe as that seemed very far from Loch Broom in those days, but I did see the convoys sailing away to the north – well outside the Summer Isles – when accompanying Uncle Alec on his lobster fishing trips.

In my mind, I clearly see these ships in convoy and on their way north with black plumes of smoke spiralling from their funnels and great barrage balloons flying overhead.

Me, excited as I was to see so many ships, happily pointing them out to my uncle, himself a survivor of an even more brutal war.

He, shaking his head sadly at the grand sight, knowing in his wisdom that many of these vessels would never return to these shores, and knowing that so many of their brave and hardy crew would end up perishing far from home in an icy sea.

The captains of both merchant and naval ships would have prayed for wild weather, something they would never have done in times of peace.

Wild weather they could endure, but attacks by enemy planes and submarines was an entirely different matter. A storm might keep the enemy at bay.

AT LOCH EWE

Soon the convoy would sail and last-minute items were being sent to the ships by local tenders, hired by the Navy. One such was "Senorita", a Loch Fyne skiff from Ullapool and crewed for the duration by local men. Perhaps it was she which transported the strongly built box marked "Urgent" and "Secret", out to a waiting destroyer to be delivered to Murmansk.

This box was duly hoisted aboard and lashed down on the vessel's deck. So important was this item that special attention was paid to its every movement. Hopefully, the lashings would hold it in position during a stormy passage – but did they?

It was not unusual in this time of war to find interesting items washed up on the shore. These perhaps spoke of tragedies at sea, but for the finders, they were hopefully things of use and so the communities along the shoreline made a habit of keeping a lookout for these seaborne treasures.

It came about that a badly bruised wooden box was spotted bumping over the rocks among other debris, and it was eventually washed up on the beach at Polglas. As ever, the finders of the box approached the item with great caution, waiting until the tide had gone back, leaving the box high and dry.

It did not look dangerous but you never could tell. They wondered what this sturdy box might contain. Who among them would dare to prise up the heavily nailed boards? It was suggested that it was their civic duty to open the box, but they also knew it was their *actual* duty to report it to the Coastguard or the Receiver of Wreck. But such a person did not exist in that area and now that one bold man had appeared with a spade, well... the heavy planks of the box were soon prised up and the contents revealed.

Glory-be!

The excited locals found wealth aplenty in the shape of thousands of tightly bound, newly minted, bank notes. So well had they been protected by waxed-paper that they rustled crisp and dry to the touch, and indeed they could easily be confused with pound notes being the same colour and same size.

Ah! But alas, to their great disappointment they bore Chinese or some-such lettering.

As mentioned, the matter should have at least

been reported to some authority.

But, what the heck! Now, with wads of cash in their hands, surely it would be better to say nothing about it and instead divide the loot amongst the community, thus sharing the wealth – but also the responsibility for the decision taken.

Thus Achiltibuie became rich.

At school on the Monday morning, we local schoolboys noticed the Achiltibuie lads coming in with an even more jaunty air than usual – as if they had come up in the world somehow. And on seeing that I had a brand new pencil, Donnie wondered, if, by any chance, I might wish to sell it to him?

I was surprised.

'Where in the world would you have the money to buy such a pencil?' I asked.

He stood up, and turning slightly away he reached into his jacket pocket and fished out a wad of notes and peeling off a couple he threw them down on my desk, saying in a lordly tone, 'Would that cover it?'

Without further ado, a deal was struck and the secret of the riches was out. OK, I had lost my brand new pencil but, in Chinese terms, I felt quite rich, moreover, Lord Donnie graciously allowed me to have his old pencil – worn down to an inch as it was and heavily engraved with his own teeth marks.

CONCLUSION

I feel that, although some of this Chinese currency did escape into the community at large, there must still be stacks of the stuff squirrelled away in the old houses of Achiltibuie. And there is the hope, now that China is on the up and up, that one day Lord Donnie will be rich once more.

A Holy Handshake

....

Dear reader, it is not my intention to remind you of your history lessons as you may well know more of this subject than I do.

That said, in this story, there is a strong connection between the bloody battle which took place, quite near to us at Culloden Moor, and our own settlements at Lochbroom – and in particular, Clachan.

It was 1746. The battle was over, but there had been a fearful loss of life and the moor at Culloden was now strewn with the dead, both Jacobite and Government soldiers.

The Duke of Cumberland, jubilant at his speedy victory over an ill-armed and disordered army, was anxious to clear the field of abandoned weapons and the mortal remains of his own soldiers – as well as those of the Jacobite rebels – and had had pits dug wherein the dead, and the nearly dead, were unceremoniously laid. Orders were issued to march their prisoners to Inverness, to be held in what was then known as the Gaelic church and which is now Leakey's Bookshop.

These prisoners, some of them fit, but some suffering terrible battle wounds must have wondered what would happen to them. They were quite soon to find out. The more seriously wounded were removed from the church, not for medical attention, but to face the executioner in the yard behind.

There can still be seen, in the graveyard behind the church, a low stone – this does not, as you may think, mark a grave. No. This stone has a chiselled groove across which the weary marksman, inured to his task, would lay his musket and take aim at his trembling target, standing blindfolded against the high boundary wall.

There, one after the other, life ended.

As time went on, the remaining prisoners were selected and marched from the church to the harbour where they were put into coastal-craft which ferried them to prisons throughout the country.

It was a government requirement, however, that all able prisoners should be shipped to the colonies as slave labour. Thus it was, that many were held in the prison ships anchored off Gravesend in the Thames, waiting to be transported to, perhaps, the West Indies.

Clachan Church stands at the head of Loch Broom and has been a centre of spirituality for a thousand years or more. In those days it was the Parish Church of Lochbroom and at times of worship, it would be crowded to the rafters with all the people of the parish, especially when the Reverend James

Robertson was appointed Minister.

For the Reverend Robertson life at Clachan proved to be good – there was a strong congregation and a large area of glebe land. Here he could farm, grow crops, and raise sheep and cattle.

Fishing rights also went with the glebe, both on the river and in the loch – and let us not forget the fish traps which can still be seen at the head of the loch – there shoals of herring were caught.

All this made the ministry at Clachan financially comfortable.

As you will find out he was a very good man, beloved by his parishioners, and here he remained from May 1745 until his death in 1776.

In my mind's eye, I try to imagine what this man looked like. It is well known that he was referred to as "the Strong Minister", so perhaps he may have been tall and broad with an air of great strength – this would have been much admired in those days of hard physical work, and I think would still be nowadays.

Also, in his personal character he was said to be forthright and eloquent, anyway the congregation heartily approved of him, especially as he, in his enthusiastic way, worked alongside them on the land and in the fisheries.

But I will depart from the main story for a moment to tell you a little tale which might show an even more human side to this man.

At the time of a service of worship in the church, it was usual for the congregation to take their places and then, after they were settled, the minister would enter. On this particular day, the minister strode down from the manse expecting everyone to be already inside, and indeed most were, but a number of older boys were still milling about the entrance.

Little attention was paid by the boys to the approach of Reverend Robertson.

He was surprised.

'What are you doing here? Are you not going in?' he asked.

'Later,' they said, 'when we have finished playing this game.'

'What game would that be then, boys?'

They explained that they were competing over who could throw this heavy stone the furthest – to see who was the strongest.

The minister looked at the stone.

'That's a very heavy stone, who is the champion?'

The boys answered that Rory was by far the best, indeed, he could throw it about twenty feet.

'Well, well,' said the minister and picking up the stone and standing on the mark, he swung back his arm and chucked the stone high and long, more than doubling Rory's twenty feet. And without another word, he turned his back on the boys and continued into the church.

The boys followed sheepishly along behind.

Anyway, back to the story in hand.

The minister and his parishioners stood to sing and, given these times of conflict, it was appropriate perhaps that the first psalm sung was Psalm No. 46 which contains these words:

> *He makes wars cease*
> *to the ends of the earth.*
> *He breaks the bow and shatters the spear.*

For now indeed, there was conflict in the land.

The Stuarts, exiled as they were in France, were anxious to regain the throne and Bonnie Prince Charlie arrived on our shores looking for recruits to fight on his behalf. The young men signed up enthusiastically. They were seeking adventure and were easily seduced by promises of betterment and wealth, and in the passion and fervour of the moment maybe they thought it would be an easy fight.

But Reverend Robertson was not happy.

He did not approve of the uprising and he lost many boys from his congregation. He thought of them as innocents and wished for them to stay out of harm's way and instead peacefully work the crofts and land at home, however, there was not much he could do to stop them marching off to war.

News of the Jacobite disaster was slow to reach Lochbroom, even though in modern terms it is only an hour away. A few, despite Cumberland's soldiers seeking them out, made it back. By hiding out, here and there, in caves, they hoped that soon the search would be over and that they could return home to their families.

It was learned, eventually, that a number of the Lochbroom men who had been imprisoned would never again see their homeland. They had been transported off from Inverness to Gravesend, to the prison ship, there to be shipped off to the colonies as slaves.

I suppose that it may have been some kind of relief for those at home to know that their young men were at least still alive and not lying dead in the cold earth of Culloden field. But, of course, they yearned to have them back again and they appealed to their Minister for help, and he, painfully aware of his people's distress, promised to do all he could to persuade the authorities to release them.

The Reverend Robertson was doubtful if his appeal would be successful, but he agreed to journey to London and seek an interview with the great Duke of Cumberland.

After a long journey south, he eventually arrived in London, there to confront the mighty Cumberland. He surely must have felt a tremor of fear as his hired carriage rolled up at the Duke's magnificent residence whereupon he duly stepped out.

A lonely figure he must have cut, but he would have hidden it well, tall and strong as he was.

Demanding to see the great man as a matter of urgency, he was made to wait an hour or more before eventually being shown into an opulent room where Cumberland himself sat behind a large desk.

The Sergeant at Arms announced, 'My Lord, this is the Reverend James Robertson of Lochbroom.'

Cumberland arose and came forward to greet the Minister. And with a rather patronising tone, he said, 'Well, Minister, you are a long way from home, are you not? What can I do for you?'

Robertson stood stiff and stern, and looking straight into Cumberland's face replied, 'I am a long way from home, Sir, but my demand is simple. You have young men from my congregation in your prison ships here. I wish for them to be released.'

'Well now, Minister, thank you for your request, but the answer is quite simply – no. They are enemies of the King and, as such, they will be deported. They are indeed fortunate to be still alive!'

With this closing remark, he extended his hand to

the Minister, signalling that the interview was over, and to bid him a good journey back to Lochbroom.

This act was his undoing.

The Minister took Cumberland's hand with a gentle and friendly grip and staring deep into Cumberland's eyes suggested that even at this late stage in their interview he might change his mind. The mighty, hard-working hand then squeezed the pen-pushing, paw of Cumberland ever more tightly.

Cumberland, ever conscious as he was of keeping up appearances, and under the watchful eye of the Sergeant-at-Arms and others present in the room, was now trying vainly to recover it whilst keeping a smile on his face.

With the bones of his hand cracking in pain and sweat breaking out on his brow, Cumberland finally had to give ground.

Through clenched teeth, he suggested that he might look into the Minister's request.

'Have I your word on it, Cumberland?' growled the Minister, exerting just a little more pressure.

'You have my word, Minister. They will be sent home... and hopefully, you will go with them.'

Thus ended the interview.

THE AFTERMATH

True to his word, "Butcher Cumberland" issued a notice of release in favour of the men in captivity at Gravesend, and arrangements were made for the prisoners to be returned to Inverness and thence home.

James Robertson made haste to return to his beloved parish where he was greeted with love and affection by his congregation, grateful that he had brought back the sons of Lochbroom. Sons that they had thought were lost to them forever.

No-one questioned the Minister on what means of persuasion he had used in order to so successfully conclude his interview with Cumberland – he was "the Strong Minister" after all.

In their eyes he was capable of anything.

But *if* asked, he merely suggested that a friend, who had given strength to his plea, had had a hand in it.

Arthur and the Seal

....

When Arthur bought the small fishing boat he had dreams of making his fortune, but as he would begin to find out, dreams do not necessarily turn out, do they?

His target was lobster which the previous owner of the "Lucy" assured him were so abundant that a couple of seasons would see the boat paid off.

Well, for Arthur, it would prove different.

Certainly, it was more challenging than working on the rigs which was what he had been doing during the past five years. Of course, it was this work that had enabled him to save the goodly sum of cash that the retiring owner of the Lucy had asked for.

But Arthur knew very little of fishing, or fishing boats, despite having been surrounded by the sea whilst working for the oil companies. However, he was energetic and very quick to learn and as the creels came with the boat he was soon able to get started.

The harbour master, realising that Arthur was a complete novice, was quite concerned and he proved helpful to Arthur, advising him on the safety equipment he should have in his boat.

He also cautioned him about the no-go areas in the loch – places where extra strong tides could be encountered and warned him of one location where there was a considerable whirlpool which might endanger a small boat such as the Lucy.

Arthur heeded his advice and was very careful for the first few weeks of operations, indeed so cautious was he in keeping clear of rocky areas that he caught very few lobsters – lobsters inhabit very inhospitable waters and caution is something that must sometimes take second place in this type of fishing.

This Arthur soon began to realise, prompting him to take on ever more risk.

With caution thrown to the wind, Arthur set a fleet of creels close to the area which the harbour master had advised against – an area of strong tides – and results were immediately better. His new fishing ground was also close to the place where at certain times the menacing whirlpool appeared and, indeed, it was here that Arthur got into trouble.

He had thrown out the last creel of a fleet of fifteen and was turning his boat towards deeper, safer waters when the blue creel rope, still buoyant as it was, caught the blades of the revolving propeller.

In his inexperience, he was slow to realise this and the first he knew of it was the slowing down of the engine before it came to a complete stop. The Lucy now swung round, stern on to the sea, anchored hard and fast by the heavy fleet of creels.

'Uh, what should I do now?' wondered Arthur.

Luckily he was in no immediate danger as there was not much wind at present, so he set to and worked on with getting free and clear of the creels, whilst also keeping a close eye on the rocks which lurked just below the surface.

He was a resourceful man, and wielding the boat hook he picked up a bight of the offending rope and pulled, but with no effect.

'There must be a hundred turns around the prop,' he muttered to himself, 'Perhaps if I turn the shaft by hand I'll free it.'

This he did, turning the shaft within the boat in the astern direction. All that happened was that some rope was released, but some more was wound on. This was no use at all and he cursed aloud in his frustration.

Looking down over the stern and through the sea, he could see the propeller entangled and ensnared by the blue rope. He reached down knife in hand, but he could barely reach the water level, never mind the propeller.

Strange that this clever fellow did not think of lashing his knife to the boat hook. But no, tricks such as these are learned through years of experience and it was in this one area that he was lacking. Perhaps if he had had another person with him this obvious course of action might have occurred to one or the other, but no, he was all on his own and now in a fix.

'I'll have to get into the water,' he thought, 'Good thing I've got the drysuit with me.'

He proceeded to kit himself out in his drysuit,

which a diver friend on the rigs had given to him.

Now suitably clad, Arthur lowered himself over the gunwale and, with one hand on the rudder to steady himself, he began to hack away at the tangle of rope surrounding the propeller.

He had to duck his head beneath the surface of the water to get close enough, only coming up for a gasp of air when his lungs were truly at their limit.

Gradually, with much effort, the knife cut away the entangling rope.

But then... disaster.

Arthur did the most stupid of things. He cut the last strand of rope so that now the boat was free of the creels, but as soon as she was free she began to drift off in the freshening breeze and Arthur lost his grip on the slimy rudder. He couldn't reach the gunwale to pull her back and in a moment the Lucy and Arthur were yards apart, the boat being blown in one direction, and Arthur being carried along on the strong tide in another.

'Hell, I've done it now!' exclaimed Arthur, watching in dismay as the breeze carried the Lucy away from him. He saw her bumping hard and scraping against the juts of jagged rock poking above the surface of the sea, whilst he himself was being drawn along more and more quickly in the opposite direction by the strengthening current.

'If only I could get ashore,' he said anxiously to himself, looking up at the sea cliff rising steep and sheer from the water to a dizzying height – perhaps a hundred feet or more.

It looked to be impossible.

This was not a word that Arthur liked, or indeed much used.

He did not panic, and in the drysuit, he was reasonably warm despite the coldness of the sea.

The only thing to do, he thought, was to let the tide carry him along to where he might see a landing place and from there he could scramble ashore and walk overland to summon help. Perhaps with a bit of luck, they might recover the boat before she got smashed up on the rocks.

By now Arthur was getting into real trouble.

He began to have an inkling of the danger that he might be in when he heard, ahead of him, the dull roar of swirling water. The ever-increasing flow of the tide had caused the whirlpool to form and Arthur found himself in a rip of water rushing towards its turbulent eye.

Helpless in the midst of it he was completely out of control and, for the first time, he was very frightened.

As he was swept deeper into that black hole his life seemed to be fast disappearing, and he found himself thinking... is this my end?

MISSING

At the harbour, fellow fisherman noticed that the Lucy was not yet in and, with evening approaching, they began to worry.

The harbour master asked around if anyone had seen anything of Arthur during the day. One of the men said that he thought he had seen the Lucy working on the north side of the loch.

Even though the weather had been good during the day the harbour master, knowing full well of the extent of Arthur's experience – or lack thereof – was most concerned.

'I think someone must go out and have a look for him. Perhaps he has broken down,' he said, although a voice within was suggesting a rather more serious outcome – the north side, after all, was where the whirlpool was.

Well, he reasoned to himself, he won't have gone there. Had he not warned the man, only last week, to keep clear of that place?

John Campbell's fast boat was sent out to search the north side for signs of Arthur, and they were not half an hour away when they radioed back that they had picked up the boat near the high rocks on the north side, but that there was no sign of Arthur; however, they would continue their search of each and every rocky inlet along the shoreline.

They all knew that this would be a difficult task and already their hopes had begun to fade.

In waters such as these, it does not take long before hypothermia sets in, and that is supposing that he had not already drowned.

In his mind, the harbour master saw Arthur swirling down into the whirlpool.

He alerted the coastguard and before long the helicopter arrived to assist in the search for the missing man. Firstly for a living body, but as time went on – a corpse. But of either, not a trace was found. The Lucy was towed back by John Campbell's boat and eventually, after the whole loch was scoured, the search was scaled down. Fellow fishermen shook their heads and muttered sadly, 'He must have gone overboard.'

This he had.

'The whirlpool's got him,' they said.

And so it had.

When Arthur regained consciousness he couldn't make anything out – pitch black as it was. He could hear, but faintly, the gentle lapping of the sea. Groping around he concluded that he had been washed ashore. His body ached all over, but as far as he could tell nothing seemed to be broken.

How lucky, he thought, when morning comes I'll be able to see my way out of here.

Painfully, he dragged his bruised and battered body higher up onto the shore, and feeling his way in this dark void he found a place offering a small amount of comfort – a thick mat of dry seaweed that had been washed up at the high water mark.

There he lay back to rest his weary frame and, exhausted as he was, he quickly fell asleep.

Awakening, Arthur's eyes adjusted to the gloom, and as time went on some light – glowing up through the water – made him vaguely aware that he was in some sort of sea cave. Getting stiffly to his feet in the brightening light, he cast his eyes about him, finding to his great dismay that this was indeed a cave, but one with no inlet or outlet except through the sea.

Looking intently down through the water he could see a passage out – fifty feet or more below the surface – and there large, fat pollock swam around lazily, comfortable and at ease in their world.

Whilst he was a reasonable swimmer he knew that he could never swim to that depth, never mind hope to make his escape through the rocky tunnel.

He was trapped and he knew it.

He wondered how long he had been there. And what time it could be. The only clue to the passing of time was the light filtering up through the water.

'I wonder if there's a search on for me?' he asked the pollock.

'Although there is not much chance of finding me in this place,' he added hopelessly.

As long as the dim light lasted Arthur searched his prison. The cave was large and deep with a high rocky ceiling and the floor was covered in a layer of flat rocks, shingle, and sand. Above the high water mark was the thick carpet of seaweed he had slept upon, presumably drawn in and then forced up through the entrance by the whirlpool, just as he himself had been.

A trickle of water was coming through the rock at the back of the cave which, upon tasting, he discovered to be cool and fresh.

At least I'll not die of thirst, he thought, with some relief, but what about food?

The very thought of food suddenly brought on gnawing pangs of hunger, but there was nothing to eat in the cave but for the fish. And the fish? Well, they were far out of reach.

The drysuit had kept him warm, but a sudden call of nature demanded its removal, it was then that he discovered the box of matches in his pocket.

Perhaps I can get a fire going, he thought; there are plenty of dry twigs and stuff above the tideline, and a fire will cheer the place up.

The match flared and the gathered kindling caught surprisingly easily, lighting up the cavern but only further revealing to the imprisoned man his awful predicament; not a crack could be seen in the rocky walls.

Indeed, the absence of any outlet was causing an

immediate problem as the smoke from the fire was now filling the place.

Soon, coughing and with eyes streaming, he kicked the fire apart and collapsed in despair. He would die here and nobody would ever know what had become of him.

FOOD

Shuffling and panting noises in the gloom awoke him and he sat up in alarm. What new disaster was this? Eyes straining he could just about make out some creature emerging from the water.

Could this be the rescue party?

Hope plummeted as he realised that the new arrival was but a seal, and, hidden as he was in the murky shadows of the cave, he watched as she hauled her herself heavily from the water onto the sloping rock, with a still-struggling fish flapping from her mouth.

He shuffled nearer to the seal and, strangely, although the animal was obviously aware of him it showed no indication of alarm except that she dropped the fish which, seizing its own opportunity to escape, began to flip flap back down the slope to the sea.

Arthur lunged at the slippery meal, catching it before it reached the water.

'Got you!'

'Ah! Food at last.'

He sank his teeth into the still living fish.

He realised, on his first bite of food in what may have been days, that fish tastes better when cooked, and so set about relighting the fire.

His godsent provider, the seal, slipped silently

away into the dark lagoon.

The smoke had once more so filled the cave that the hungry man was forced to extinguish the flames. With his throat rasping and his eyes burning, he drew from the embers the blackened, but still raw, remains of the fish.

He retreated to the water's edge, as far as possible from the smoke, and although the delicious smell belied the reality – he tore at the flesh greedily.

This, he brooded, may be my last meal of all time.

Lying back on the sand, his mind wandered over the trouble that had so recently befallen him.

He thought, with gratitude, of the arrival of the seal, the provider of this life-giving, if not particularly well-cooked, fare. It would seem highly unlikely that such a miracle could happen again.

So, despite his now contented stomach, the future seemed sombre indeed.

THE RETURN OF THE SEAL

It was several hours later that the seal came back, but even though this time there was no offering of fish Arthur was glad to have the company of this gentle creature. The seal too seemed to want to be near Arthur and came to rest close to where he lay.

Indeed so close, that Arthur reached out and touched the silky smooth fur of his companion. He'd heard that seals have a most dreadful bite and yet he felt quite safe, and as he stroked the animal he realised that she felt safe too.

Her head rose up to look at him.

And she gently rolled her eyes.

This simple expression was so human that he almost cried out. Indeed, he recalled his mother's eyes rolling heavenward in exactly the same way on finding her child in a fix of his own making.

As though he was explaining his predicament to his mother Arthur explained it to the seal, stroking the animal whilst he did so. The seal, with those almost human eyes, murmured back to him and soon he began to realise that she really *was* trying to communicate with him.

'What are you trying to tell me, girl, eh?' he asked.

With ever more urgency she flung up her head and barked.

'I know what you're trying to tell me. You're suggesting that it's time I took myself off home. Well, I would, if I could swim like you.'

The seal, perhaps not understanding Arthur's inadequacies as a swimmer, tried to reinforce her message by flapping her flippers.

'Look, I've got the message, I've overstayed my welcome, but how do you propose to get rid of me?'

The seal laid her head back down, almost as if she had understood what Arthur had been saying and now needed to think about it, but then, and very much to Arthur's surprise, she farted loudly.

'Damn it all, old girl,' said Arthur, recoiling from the sickening stench of rotting fish, 'I get the message.'

On moving quickly away from his stinky friend he came across a piece of creel rope, half buried in the shingle at the edge of the cave.

A mad idea occurred to him and he muttered, 'I wonder if she could swim me out under tow?'

Approaching the seal and holding up the rope he said, 'I'll tie one end around me and the other end around you. How about that?'

He fitted a neat loop around himself, all the while

keeping an eye on the seal and talking about his plan. The seal, watching with interest, nodded her head and began to slide quickly towards the water.

'Hey! Not so fast, girl!' exclaimed Arthur, hastily splicing the small loop for the seal's end.

The seal slipped into the water.

'Oh, blast!' said Arthur, 'She's gone.'

But no – her head bobbed up at the water's edge and she barked at him once more, as if she were waiting rather impatiently for Arthur to finish what he was doing and get a move on.

Arthur completed the loop and knelt down with a pounding heart and slipped the loop over her head.

I'm nuts, he thought, this will never work.

Man and animal were now umbilically connected and the seal, perhaps sensing Arthur's second thoughts, seized control. She whirled around and with the speed of an arrow being released from a bow, she dived away.

The rope tightened around him and he shot down the slippery slope into the icy water. Gulping one instinctive – and maybe final – gasp of air, Arthur and the seal dove down into the deep water of the lagoon. So quickly did this all happen that he had not a moment to panic.

Down and down they went until the seal levelled off, whereupon they entered the tunnel. Dragging him through, Arthur was scraped painfully along under the ceiling rocks of the cave's mouth.

But finally, up-up-up they went, ascending quickly through the streaming fingers of light in the water, before finally piercing through the surface itself into this other world of blinding sun and air.

Like a newborn, he gasped for breath.

Free!

Man and animal bobbed together on the calm water, Arthur babbling words of gratitude that the animal had no way of understanding. The huge, liquid, black orbs that were the seal's eyes, looked deep into Arthur's own. In his mind she seemed to be telling him that he was safe now, and that she must be gone. Arthur reached out and gently removed the rope that had linked them on this short, but life giving journey.

The seal did not immediately leave Arthur; instead, she circled slowly around him, keeping her eyes upon him – as if to make sure that he was indeed safe and well.

Arthur solemnly thanked her from the bottom of his heart, and this the seal appeared to understand, as finally she left him. Spiralling gracefully away and down she disappeared into the indigo waters.

He had no wish to endanger himself again, so he began to swim towards deeper water, away from the rocky shoreline, in the hope that some passing fishing boat would pick him up.

By the look of the day and the position of the sun, it was late afternoon – the prawn fishermen should be heading for harbour before too long.

THE HARBOUR

At around 5 p.m. the harbour master was astounded to receive a VHF call from Sammy MacLean on the "Happy Hour". Arthur had been picked up at Càrn Nan Sgeir, alive and well. Although he was raving on and on about being saved by some seal.

It took the fishing boat the best part of an hour to

reach the harbour and in that time Arthur, listening in as Sammy MacLean and his crewman discussed his condition, decided that there was no way the story of the seal was going to be believed.

He made up his mind that he would keep quiet about it, and so it was that, when helped ashore at the pier and with the landing place thronged with curious well-wishers, Arthur feigned amnesia.

'No, I can't remember a thing,' he muttered.

'Oh, you're a lucky devil, eh!' said the fishermen, shaking their heads in wonder at Arthur's survival.

After all the fuss had died down, Arthur got rid of the Lucy and was soon back doing a job that he knew better. It was there, whilst sharing a night shift on the rig, that he told me his story.

I believe every word of it.

Well, would *you* not?

The Hens, Our Friends

. . . .

In my childhood, we lived at Craigmore on Shore Street and my family – like most other households in the village – had hens.

They were just a part of our lives; regularly presenting us with eggs each day and at the end of their lives providing the family with a wholesome meal – unlike the blotting paper, now sold in the shops, that passes itself off as chicken.

As children, did we like hens?

No, we did not.

Our hens wandered freely everywhere.

Not having dedicated premises for themselves, into our workshop they went, depositing their droppings, without any shame, on all our precious things.

That was the way of life then.

Outdoors and indoors merged in a way that is no longer acceptable.

Nowadays it is a different matter, and the "in thing" is to have hens as your friends.

We build them comfortable residences – maybe some form of heating would be nice we think, and maybe a little window they could peep out from – to help them decide whether or not to go forth and stretch their legs of a morning, before partaking in a nutritious breakfast; this meal duly provided by an adoring owner who wishes only to have a little chat with them – an exchange of friendly little clucks.

In return for all this love is the joy of finding the wondrous gift of a golden-yoked egg or two.

And on assuring ourselves that all is well within our little fowl community, we will hasten to our place of work, or our home, and compare notes with our fellow hen lovers.

The huge difference now is the calmness of the little fowl family. The modern critters go about gently chook-chook-chooking amongst themselves.

I ask you, dear people, where are the strident pre-dawn crowings of old? Where is the strutting magnificence of the proud Cockerel ruling the roost in his appointed community?

I should mention that, at that time we lived next door to the Youth Hostel which for many years was run by the much loved, ever smiling and twinkly-eyed Dina Lawson.

Did Dina appreciate the raucous 5 a.m. wake up call from our splendid bird?

Doubtful.

But laughing, she countered my father's embarrassed apology saying, 'Never mind, Willie, it gets them up and out, nice and early.'

Meaning, of course, her formerly slumbering residents.

Which reminds me of a tale I heard back then of a hen keeper at Ardmair.

A very serious man, and the proud owner of a splendid bird, Randolph. This man, being of an upright nature, was concerned that Randolph's – or rather, Randy's, as he was fondly known – ear splitting morning calls might be causing offense on the Sabbath. (Along with some other more dubious antics which may be considered by many to be most unseemly, but especially so on the seventh day).

In consequence, he announced to his dear wife that, in future, Randy should be placed under a basket on Saturday p.m. and left there until Monday a.m..

The regime was introduced but was soon discontinued when it was noticed that not only was Randy suffering in ignominy under his prison of a basket but that his deprived spouses had gone into a decline, refusing their food and not laying any eggs.

'I told you,' said his wife, 'that this would be a mistake. After all, how would you feel under similar circumstances?'

The man admitted that 'it would be *unthinkable*.'

The basket was lifted without further ado.

And Randy, being now – free as a bird – as they say, crowed as he had never crowed before.

Indeed, his joyful, boastful chants could be heard from Rhue to Strathkanaird.

The hens were happy once more and the gift of eggs resumed.

They were so proud of their Lord Randolph.

And more importantly, Lord Randolph was proud of Lord Randolph – it is incumbent on one of his gender and species after all.

Have you ever heard of a humble cockerel?

Probably not.

The moral of this story?

Because, of course, there must be one.

Well, ladies, it is this – appreciate the male ingredient in life.

Oh, and I say: 'bring back that early morning cock-crowing chorus!'

It was not perhaps melodic or tuneful, but it is a sound that is reminiscent of childhood and happy days gone by.

What if?

....

Aboard our ship, the RRS Shackleton, we were leaving Southampton and heading south, down the Atlantic to eventually arrive at Antarctica, calling at Recife, Montevideo, and finally the Falkland Islands and Port Stanley where we would be based.

Each day the weather improved, now came gentle breezes and warm sunshine. Taking advantage of these conditions, the second and third mates, in their free time, began to take an interest in a clinker-built rowing boat that had been left aboard by the previous Norwegian owner of our ship. These two young fellows planned to improve the craft so that they could sail her when we reached Port Stanley.

A mast and sails became available and plans were drawn up by the two enthusiastic sailors.

They required lots of bits and pieces to be manufactured in the engine room, and it was there that they found me. I had little enthusiasm for the project but I listened to the improvements planned for this, quite ordinary, fourteen-foot rowing boat.

I listened and wondered.

However, as an engineer, I had no say in their design, but I did help them by making whatever they wanted.

These "improvements" to the boat would, I was assured, increase her sailing performance.

We'll see,' I said cautiously, hearing of their intention to add a nine-inch plank to her existing keel.

'Oh, she'll go like the wind,' they said in perfect unison and with total confidence.

On arrival at Port Stanley our ship was moored up to a T-shaped pier and, as the ship was much longer than the pier, our vessel provided additional shelter for smaller boats like the rowing boat now being improved by the mates – with the mast and the rigging and...

Oh, no!... that nine-inch addition to the keel.

When all was complete, my friends – thinking back to the person who had made the few bits and pieces – thought that I might wish to join them in the first sea trials. Maybe I should have declined the invitation, but I did not.

Seeing that the weather was now cold and windy, which is pretty typical for that place, I proceeded to kit myself out in layers of my warmest gear and after donning sea boots – and looking somewhat like a penguin – I waddled down to the foreshore where the boat lay ready rigged. I still remember stepping aboard this cranky tub, (there is a Gaelic word describing such a craft – *corrach* – meaning unstable) I should have stepped ashore right there and then, but you don't, do you? And so, despite my misgivings, I took my place in the boat.

As I said, the ship's length provided a certain amount of shelter in its lee and this was welcome now that the wind had increased. With a certain amount of alarm, I suggested to the mates that they should confine the trials to the more sheltered area provided by the overhanging ship, as there the sea was fairly calm, and they agreed to this while promptly raising the sail.

Feeling the wind in the sail, this wee *corrach* boat rushed ahead like a dog after a bone. Vainly the helmsman attempted to spill the wind, but the boat would not answer to the helm – listening only to the effect of her new keel which made her quite unable to turn.

'Drop the sail!' I shouted.

No joy!

The sail was stuck fast at the masthead and so we flew away past the sheltering stern and out into the choppy water of the bay, all the while, but vainly, we attempted to get this improved boat under control.

The end was in sight.

Now out in the deeps, she began to ship water over her starboard gunwale. I, being forward, made ready to leave this now flooding craft and as she finally filled and fell over to starboard I slipped into the freezing water from the port side, while the mates, being aft, struggled out from under the rogue mainsail which was sealing them below the surface.

Three men *not* in a boat!

In theory, we should have been able to hang on to the boat; it being wood it would not sink, and it didn't; instead, because of the stuck sail and the wind on the choppy water the boat continued to flip over and over with the risk of us being either trapped under the sail, or being brained by the flailing mast and spars.

Things were looking bleak.

None of us was equipped for this.

In those days I considered myself to be an able swimmer and thought that I could make it to the now distant shore. I would have to at least get my sea boots off and, kicking hard, I managed to struggle out of one – but unfortunately not the other – making my condition even worse for the long swim back. Anyhow, conversation with my fellow sufferers suggested that we should all stick together, which we did, and which was right.

I was twenty-five then, an age at which one considers oneself to be pretty indestructible; that being said, I had to admit that unless something good should happen soon, the wedding my fiancée and I had planned for August might not happen.

What if the groom failed to appear?

My bride might be left at the altar.

Oh, dear.

On looking back to where our ship was moored we observed some movement aboard – frantic attempts were being made to launch a lifeboat.

Oh, joy! They were aware of our predicament!

Help was on its way!

Or was it?

We three sodden, and soon to be frozen, mariners watched in amazement at their cack-handed efforts to launch the lifeboat. It was now hanging grotesquely on end with her bow nosing into the sea and her stern still attached to the lowering falls.

Despite our very own cack-handed efforts which had brought us to this sad predicament, we laughed scornfully, shouting insults to the distant lifesavers.

Oh, the impudence of these three young fellows!

Fortunately, and unknown to us, a small workboat lay at the pier and it was this brave little vessel, pressed into service by the local islanders, which soon arrived to fish out three very relieved would-be sailors.

Oh, what a shambles!

P.S. The groom did appear at the appointed time, thus allowing a wedding to take place – resulting in the creation of seven 'Nabbie' like creatures. A ready and mostly willing audience for my tales!

The Stone

. . . .

The boy and his mother relaxed in the warm
sunshine, she sitting in a chair in the doorway of the
house, he playing with a little toy on the doorstep.
They enjoyed each other's company and had a great
understanding of one another.

'Oh, isn't it a lovely day, Tommy?' she said, fondly
running her fingers through the golden curls of the
child's hair. 'Look, dear, I think that's your Aunty
Kate coming to see us.'

The boy raised his eyes from his toy and gazed
at the distant figure making her way towards them.
She always called on them when in the village, but of
late these visits were fewer. She was finding the long
walk from the croft a strain and, of course, the walk
back was even worse, up that steep brae carrying her
heavy messages and all.

The bright sun made it necessary for the mother

and child to shade their eyes with their hands as they watched her slowly making her way down the road.

The child took a stone out of his pocket, a small flat pebble with a hole in the centre. Since finding this stone on the shore it had become one of his most treasured possessions.

'Look, Mother,' he said eagerly, 'if I look through the stone I can see much better!'

The mother laughed, her child was so observant. 'Just like a monocle, I suppose.'

'Do you know, Mother, I think I can see someone with her.'

'Nonsense,' she said, 'you are screwing up your eyes too tightly. Put that stone away and run to meet your aunt.'

The boy dutifully pocketed the stone and ran up the road to greet her, taking her hand and walking back with her towards his waiting mother.

'Oh, Kate,' exclaimed the mother, 'you are looking tired. Come and sit down here and we'll have a cup of tea. Go in, Tommy, and put the kettle on.'

The sisters sat together and after a while Tommy returned, carefully carrying a tray laden with teacups and saucers, and the steaming teapot filled with a refreshing brew for the ladies.

'My, what a grand boy you have there, Jessie,' said Aunt Kate approvingly.

The boy then piped up, 'Aunty Kate, do you know I saw two of you coming down the road when I was looking at you through my stone.'

The sisters laughed.

'What stone is that then?' questioned Kate.

He gave her the stone and she and Jessie examined it with great interest, looking through the hole and chuckling at the fun of it.

'Well, well,' said Kate, 'it does nothing for my eyesight, but it's a bonnie, wee stone.'

Handing it back to the child with a wink and a warm smile, she said, 'Tell me, Tommy, who was it that you saw with me?'

The boy thought for a moment before replying.

'Well, Aunty, the other person was just like you, but not as clear. She was more like a shadow, but not one on the ground. A shadow walking beside you.'

The two women glanced at one another.

The day suddenly seemed cooler.

'Let's go into the house, Kate. I think we are losing the sun.'

Moving into the cosy living room the amiable nature of their conversation resumed and they passed on snippets of news that they had heard. Jessie then expressed her worry about her sister living alone in the remote crofthouse, and with her not keeping well and all.

'I'll be fine, Jessie,' said Kate, 'it's just a summer cold that will not go away.'

'But, Kate, that long walk back up to the croft,' replied Jessie anxiously. 'I worry about it. It must be a killer for you!'

'On that, you need have no worry,' said Kate, 'as today it will be no problem at all. That nice Dan Robertson will be calling for me very soon. He is giving me a lift back up in his cart. He's down here for some fencing posts and suchlike.'

The afternoon wore on pleasantly – the sisters being the best of friends – and then as promised, Dan's horse and cart drew up at the front door and they took leave of one another with great fondness.

The mother and child watched as Dan helped Kate up into the cart, making her as comfortable as possible amongst the coils of wire and the neatly stacked posts. He then jumped into the front of his cart and, just as he was about to nudge his old horse forward and off, Kate leaned over and whispered worriedly in Jessie's ear:

'Perhaps, it might be better if the boy were to be rid of that stone.'

With that, the old horse pulled and the heavily laden cart slowly trundled off up the winding road.

As is the way here goodbyes can take a while, the mother and child would watch, waving from time to time, until Kate and Dan, and the horse and cart had completely disappeared from their view. Only *then* would they go back into the house.

Though now distant, they could still vaguely make out Aunt Kate sitting up on top of the cart.

Jessie waved once more.

Tommy took out his stone and looked through it.

'Do you know, Mother, I can see Aunty Kate quite clearly and look... her shadow is with her again too.'

'That's quite enough about that stone, Tommy,' said his mother severely, 'Get rid of it! Chuck it away right this minute!'

Her sister having finally gone from sight, Jessie sighed and went back in.

Tommy did not want to lose his precious stone, but to please his mother he had promised to put it away and this he did, but hidden away in a place where he would easily find it again.

Dan Robertson's horse and cart were meanwhile making their slow journey up towards the high ground where the crofts lay. Dan was walking beside the cart to help take the weight off the shoulders of the poor old horse, and as the road steepened and the horse began to snort and strain, Kate suggested that she too should get off and walk.

Dan would have none of it.

'No, no,' he said. 'Sit tight, lass, we've had bigger loads than this before now.'

Daisy, the horse, was a good-natured creature, but at this particular stage in the journey, one which she well knew, she began to get restless and rolled her eyes nervously.

She had reason to be nervous.

She sensed George MacLennan's vicious dog which, whenever it was not secured, would rush out at her, barking and snapping at her fetlocks.

Dan had not noticed Daisy's anxiety and, rather than coming to her head to lead her on, he went to the rear of the cart and pushed. At this, the steepest part of the brae, the road was only wide enough for the cart. The ground on the right-hand side plunged away down a vertiginous, boulder-strewn hillside.

The dog lay in wait.

He had heard the rumbling of the cartwheels on the gravelled road and the slow crunching and clopping of the horse's hooves, he could also hear Daisy's panting and snorting as she laboured nervously on.

The dog watched and, creeping under a bush, he waited until Daisy's head was just abreast of him before launching into her with his powerful body, barking and snapping furiously.

The terrified horse reared up and away from the maddening dog. There was nothing Dan could do to calm his terrified animal.

Over the bank went Daisy with the loaded cart still

coupled to her. Over and over they rolled, spilling the posts and wires and boards among the boulders.

Kate was screaming in terror.

Dan looked on aghast.

She was his first and only consideration.

He could see her now, lying among the wreckage of the cart and its contents, and he desperately scrambled down to where she lay, but although he could see no apparent injuries to her – indeed she seemed to be unmarked by this awful accident – he knew that she was dead. Her open eyes gazed out beyond him; beyond life itself.

Daisy too – his faithful old horse – lay dead on the rocks.

THE FUNERAL

It was awful.

Poor Dan could not be comforted.

'It was an accident, Dan,' the people said.

But he, poor soul that he was, took it all so hard, blaming himself for his inattention and after all these years of handling horses too.

The crafty crofter, George MacLennan, was quick to tell the outraged and stricken folk left behind, that he had shot the dog on the very day of the accident. This deed he hoped, would absolve him of any blame.

Jessie was beside herself with grief.

To have lost her sister and in such a way.

She kept silently asking herself – was there some dreadful connection between what had happened and that vision that her beloved child, in his innocence, had spoken of on looking through the stone?

No, no, she reassured herself, how could that be, it was just a childish fancy, sheer coincidence.

But?

For Tommy, a funeral was a new experience.

It was strange to see so many people, in their dark clothes and with their sad faces, gathered around a hole in the burial ground. He himself was dressed up in his Sunday best, and holding his mother's soft reassuring hand he wondered at the hole and at the coffin lying beside it. He found it impossible to imagine his lovely warm Aunty Kate lying in there.

'If I were to look through my stone could I see her?' he asked himself.

He had secretly slipped the stone into his pocket before leaving the house.

No-one noticed the quiet child standing among the throng of people surrounding the grave as the men, holding on to the silken chords, prepared to lower the coffin into the hole.

Tommy furtively held the stone before his eye and looked through it at the coffin, but no, he could not see her.

He scanned around.

There she was, standing nearby watching the sad crowd of people looking down into the grave.

Not absolutely clear, as she had been in life, but soft and misty.

She looked happy, he thought, and indeed, as her coffin was lowered into the ground she turned and smiled at him. As the first shovelful of black earth fell heavily upon the wooden lid, she disappeared like a wisp into the bright light.

Young though the child was, this experience confirmed to him that this stone was something very special, and to him only.

After the funeral gathering at the house was over,

and all the grieving family and friends had departed leaving the mother and son alone once more, the boy felt burdened with guilt and he knew in his heart that he must confess.

'Mother?'

The mother looked at her child.

'You remember the stone?' he said anxiously.

'Yes,' she replied sadly, 'You promised me that you would put it away. You did though, didn't you?'

'No, Mother,' uttered the child in a voice filled with shame and remorse.

And sobbing, he told her what he had seen at his aunt's funeral.

The mother held her tearful child close.

'Tommy, my dear boy,' she said, 'you have a gift. Something that is not given to many people. You can see something that others cannot. But whether it can bring happiness... Well, who can tell? Does this gift make you happy?'

'I'm not sure, Mother,' the boy said solemnly, 'Perhaps if I throw it away I'll be just like everyone else. But I do wish to keep my stone.'

Jessie thought for a while, unsure how to advise her strange child.

'Keep it for now and let us see what happens,' she said apprehensively.

Her tone brightened a little and she added, 'Though I am glad that you told me that Aunty Kate smiled. She must have found happiness in her new life, wherever that may be.'

Everything in the village returned to normal and after the summer holidays school opened, and Tommy returned there in company with his friends.

An ordinary, if quiet, child.

The stone was never discussed amongst him and his friends. He did not forget it though, and in fact, he carried it everywhere with him.

Like most boys of that time, he was glad to hear the bell at the end of the day. Pleased to heft his schoolbag onto his back and set to, off along the shore path in the company of his friends – Bobby Campbell and Hamish MacLean.

Hamish was an adventurous boy and if trouble was to be found, well he'd find it.

And so it happened this day.

It was now late in the year and the evenings were drawing in with the sky now darkening at only four o'clock. Walking home along the path the boys were surprised to see, floating at the shoreline, a rowing boat, apparently abandoned with a lot of water sloshing around in it.

'This is old Hector's boat,' said Hamish, 'it must have drifted off in the high tide.'

There were oars in the boat but no rowlocks.

'Let's take it back to Hector!' exclaimed Hamish. And jumping into it without a thought, he lifted an oar and shoved the boat out into deeper water.

His feet were now soaking wet and he realised that he should have bailed the water out. Discovering, belatedly, as he looked about him, that there was no bailer in the boat, an even worse problem showed itself – down aft the water was bubbling in.

There was no plug in the bottom.

Tommy and Bobby looked on worriedly.

'Come back to shore, Hamish!' they called.

The slowly sinking boat drifted out to sea with the offshore breeze.

With no rowlocks to put the oars in, Hamish was forced to stand up in order to paddle back. Water was now sloshing from one side to another and the boat tipped alarmingly. The boys on shore realised that their friend was in real trouble.

'Stay here, Tommy, and keep watch,' said Bobby.

And cupping his hands together he called out to his frightened friend in the boat, 'I'm going to run back to school for help!'

'Be quick! I think he's going to capsize it if he's not careful!' said Tommy.

Bobby raced off and he prayed aloud as he ran. 'Please let him make it back. Please! Please!'

Tommy remained, anxiously looking out to sea at his friend struggling and flailing with the oar.

The sky was darkening now and the boat was slipping into the dusk.

With so much water now in the boat, it rolled over and the lad was thrown into the icy cold sea. Boat and child parted company under different influences; the wind blowing the boat in one direction and the child drifting face down with the tide in another.

Mr. Stewart, the Headmaster, had come running to the rescue and was now at the shore.

Dusk had come and all they could see was the upturned boat in the distance. Hamish had, by now, completely disappeared.

The Headmaster hurriedly threw off his jacket and shoes, saying, 'I'll swim out to the boat. Hopefully, he's clinging to the gunwale.'

Tommy felt the stone in his pocket.

He slipped it out and held it up to his eye.

Almost at once his friend came into view.

'Sir!' said Tommy. 'Hamish is floating fifty yards to the left of the boat!'

Mr. Stewart looked in disbelief at the boy holding a stone to his eye, but there was no time for explanations and so he launched himself into the freezing waters of the loch and swam towards the point that Tommy had indicated.

After what seemed like an eternity Mr. Stewart found Hamish floating and turning him over he swam as strongly as he could back to the shore. As soon as he had the little body on dry land he began his efforts to resuscitate the child who, he thought, had almost certainly gone.

Bobby was sobbing with fear, but Tommy stood silently by, the stone still at his eye.

He saw Hamish lying blue on the shore.

He saw Mr. Stewart pumping his chest.

But he could also see his friend, Hamish, standing and looking anxiously over Mr. Stewart's shoulder as he tried desperately to revive the drowned child lying there.

The exhausted teacher was on the point of giving up when he felt the boy gasp.

And then, to his great joy, breathe.

Tommy, equally joyfully, watched the other Hamish fade away into the gathering darkness.

Mr. Stewart was rightly the hero of the entire community. He modestly shrugged off the praise heaped upon him by the grateful parents of Hamish. Bobby Campbell was also praised for his prompt action in running for help.

As for Tommy?

Well, there was talk, or rather whispers, of Tommy's actions, but strange to say the Headmaster never once mentioned Tommy and the service that he had rendered in saving Hamish.

Never.

Not once.

Tommy's mother knew what others did not, and was full of praise for what he had done.

'My dear,' she said with pride, 'you did well to save that boy. The gift you have could not have gone to a better person. Your poor, dead father would be so proud of you. I only wish he could see you now.'

'Perhaps he can, Mother,' said Tommy with a grin.

Sausages for Supper

As a boy, I was quite shocked to witness the brutal conduct of our local policeman as he cruelly escorted an unwilling tramp out of the village.

Dragging, as he did, this dishevelled and very bewildered individual by the none-too-clean collar of his none-too-clean coat, whilst kicking him, from time to time, about the legs, they made erratic progress towards the outer boundary of Ullapool.

Once there, the policeman abandoned him with a final kick to the backside and an aggressive warning never to return. Then, satisfied that his civic duty had been accomplished and his village had been rid of this much-despised person, he returned to enjoy a day of righteous idleness.

Once home I spoke to my parents about the incident, describing the conduct of "Rubberneck" – our local, and not too much loved, Officer of the Law.

They were very angry about it, especially my father, who had seen hard times himself in his early years after serving in the horrific trench warfare of Flanders Field.

And after the War too, he told me, there was a lot of poverty in our own country, with no work for the survivors of the conflict. No work, and so no food.

'Many a good man took to the road in dire need,' he said, 'and they should be shown respect and helped along the way, certainly not receive the treatment you witnessed!'

He often said that a tramp, upon receiving a kindness, would put a secret mark on that particular house, indicating to some other needy soul, that here he might receive civilised help.

I wondered if our house had such a mark.

I hoped that it had.

On this particular day I was alone in the house.

Father was at the shop and Mother was visiting her sister. Both would be out until late afternoon.

My instructions were to keep the place tidy, ensure the cooking range in the kitchen was kept alight and also to light the fire in the front room to provide warmth and welcome for all in the evening.

I was contemplating all these duties when I heard a loud knocking at the front door.

I hastened there to find – you've guessed it, yes, a tramp.

I could tell by his total absence of dress sense, that this was not a man about to order a new three-piece suit from my father's tailor shop. No, he was attired in what I imagined to be a tramp's uniform, casually rough, and set off by a pair of well-travelled wellies.

I remembered my father's words:

'Treat those in need with respect, and give help if possible.'

So even before my visitor had time to ask for anything I welcomed him into the house, saying, 'You'll have a cup of tea?'

I imagine that he must have been surprised at this warm welcome, but he did not show it; instead, he grunted his acceptance before then suggesting that it might be accompanied by something to eat.

I sat him down in the cosy kitchen with a mug of tea and a couple of newly baked scones. Of course, he was pleased, I could tell as I watched him tuck in, but he did not say much.

When he did finally speak his voice was hoarse and gravelly – perhaps with the dust of the road. Anyway, he seemed content to sit in the warmth of the kitchen consuming what I had provided.

I was busily building the fire up in the front room, carefully arranging the kindling and the coal which, soon enough, I would put a match to before coaxing it into life. During these ministrations, I could hear, from the sound of the floppy wellies shuffling over the linoleum floor, that my visitor was up and about in the kitchen.

My thoughts shifted back to my task and so I was startled when I heard his gruff voice coming from right behind me and saying into my ear, 'Hey, Laddie, I see a plate of sausages through there.'

'Yes,' I answered, 'that's our supper.'

'How about cooking a couple just now, afore I go on my way?' my visitor suggested.

'No.' I replied, nervously.

At his impudent request, my mother's face had suddenly appeared in a vision right before me and she wasn't smiling, so I quickly added –'Anyway, I have no knowledge of cooking at all!'

'That'll be no problem,' he growled, casting his sharp eyes around the kitchen, 'I'll show you how.'

At this, he deftly fished out my mother's cast iron frying pan, into which he then placed a couple of the precious sausages that had been planned for the evening meal.

Soon the well-tended sausages were sizzling merrily away in the hot pan, emitting a grand smell.

The kindly tramp forked one out, handing it to me, saying, 'Try that one, son.'

It was delicious.

We sat there together, each with our fork with a big, fat sausage atop.

I then went back to the front room to stoke up the fire whilst my visitor chose to remain in the kitchen, presumably tidying up after his hearty meal.

Shortly after, he joined me in the front room where the open fire was crackling away and throwing out a warming glow.

He made himself comfortable in my father's chair and placed his wellied-feet on the fender. From this position of perfect ease, the tramp became quite sociable, and talking in his husky dust-laden voice of the many journeys he had made, he was seemingly unaware that his rubber wellies were steaming and smoking and threatening to melt in the fierce heat.

The warmth of the glowing fire slowly flowed through his thin frame and his voice softened.

Then, to my astonishment, a song suddenly burst forth. He trumpeted loudly, but untunefully, a quite appropriate song for a gentleman of the road:

"The Road and Miles to Dundee"

Cauld winter was howlin',
  o'er moor and o'er mountain
And wild was the surge, of
  the dark rolling sea
When I met about daybreak,
  a bonnie young lassie,
Wha asked me the road, and
  the miles to Dundee.

Says I, my young lassie,
  I canna' weel tell ye,
The road and the distance,
  I canna' weel gie,
But if you'll permit me, tae
  gang a wee bitty,
I'll show ye the road, and
  the miles to Dundee.

It brings back warm childhood memories when I hear this song, even now. However, it was at that very moment that Mother got back.

Not such a good memory.

She could not believe what she was seeing and hearing, and it was very soon made clear that visiting time was over. My new friend shuffled hastily to the door, wafting the odour of hot, smelly wellies through the house, gone to face the lonely road once more.

Mother looked around the kitchen.

'Where are the sausages?' she asked sharply.

'Well,' I said, 'we ate two.'

She thrust an empty plate in front of me.

'And how many sausages are left on this plate?'

There were none.

As I stood, ruefully regarding the mysteriously empty plate, Father returned from work evidently looking forward to his simple meal – what with it being wartime and with rationing in full force.

'What's for supper?' he enquired.

Mother exhibited the empty plate.

Explanations were offered as to the lack of that much-looked-forward-to meal.

'...kindness to needy travellers?'

'...treat with respect?'

'...help if possible?'

All were suggested.

'Bloody tramp!' he muttered.

But then, remembering his recent advice he said, sternly: 'There are good tramps and then there are not so good tramps.'

Peat, the Great Preserver

....

The Land Rover roared up the dusty road stopping with a flourish at a group of men working at the end of a culvert. Out jumped a thin, hatchet-faced man in a wide-brimmed hat – the foreman.

'Come on up here, Paddy, me son,' he shouted down to them through the cloud of dust. (It must be said, the foreman was very fair-minded in his contempt for others; he called everyone "me son", irrespective of age, colour, religion or relationship.) 'And bring your pick and shovel with you.'

Paddy was quite pleased.

At least, he thought, if he wants me with the tools then I've still got a job.

'There's a wee job needing done up there in the hills,' said the foreman, 'Jump into the motor and we'll head up.'

As they clambered into the Land Rover he added,

'Now, it's likely you'll be up there most of the day so you'd better take your *piece* with you, as there'll be nothing to eat out there.'

Soon they were climbing up a steep track which before long petered out altogether. They continued on upwards for another mile or so until the ground flattened out onto a grassy plain. Ahead Paddy could see a red and white ranging rod staked in the boggy ground.

'Right, see that marker? I want you to dig to the hard, a hole six-foot square. Now make a tidy job of it and level out the peat that you throw out,' ordered the foreman, 'OK?'

'Whatever is the purpose of this job?' asked Paddy with interest.

'This is secret work, me son,' he replied with a hint of annoyance, 'M.O.D. So I can't be telling the likes of you too much about it. Now set to.'

In fact, he himself did not know, but he chose not to broadcast his own ignorance.

The foreman marked out the extent of the hole, not trusting Paddy with such a complicated task.

'Dig now!' he barked, 'To the hard gravel. And a tidy job I want. Remember, you're working for the British Government!'

With that last order issued he jumped back into the Land Rover and drove off, shouting out as he did so that he'd be back in the afternoon.

'Stupid idiot!' muttered Paddy picking up his shovel and shaking his head at the sheer meanness of the man.

The job would not take long, he thought – there was no need to hurry. Indeed it was a lovely day up here with the sun warm on his back, and thanks to a light breeze there was not even a midge to bother him – though he would rather be consumed by a million of those little bloodsuckers than be working under the gaze of that awful, ignorant man.

No, he was grateful to be up here on this beautiful and peaceful grassy plain, digging away on his own, miles away from that shouting foreman.

Digging peat was no problem for Paddy. In his boyhood days, back in his native land, was he not surrounded by the stuff.

So he began.

Once the spade was through the rough mat of grass and heather, the moist oily peat was like a rich black butter gleaming in the morning sun. About two feet down his shovel hit something hard, something unyielding to the sharp edge of the tool. He knew from the feel that it was not the hard gravel that he had expected.

It could be an ancient tree root, he thought.

Indeed, until a few hundred years ago, before the sheep came and nibbled everything to the ground, this land had been covered in a thick forest of rowan, pine and birch.

He paused before straightening up, reminding himself that there was no need to hurry – he had all day. But his curiosity was fired up. Ideas of what might be down there flowed through his mind. Were there not stories of people coming across buried treasure?

Huh, not much chance of that in this wilderness, he reckoned, smiling at his foolish daydream.

At the same time he could not entirely erase it from his mind and so he continued digging, but carefully, taking out dainty shovelfuls until he was down to what surely must be a stone.

Wiping away the buttery peat he saw a metal edge.
A blade?

His initial task now entirely forgotten about, he set too, delicately digging and scraping.

'Bejesus!' he exclaimed, lifting out a sword.

Placing it down on the ground he wiped the blade with a handful of rough grass. The metal shone with a soft brown gleam. The hilt too was in perfect order. And taking a few prancing steps Paddy slashed at the air with this ancient and noble weapon.

There's a bob or two in this, he thought, I've a good mind to take off here and now and to hell with the bloody hole. But, he reflected, it's a long way back to camp and that gaffer is sure to spot me, and carrying a sword too.

No.

He would finish the job he had been set. And, anyway, it had suddenly occurred to him that there may be further treasures to be found. Cautiously he resumed digging. His care was soon rewarded when the tip of his shovel snagged on what seemed to be cloth. He turned pale. A sense of foreboding came over him.

Indeed, that which was lying in the cold dark earth was a body, and from its peat-soaked, blackened appearance he knew that both the sword and its owner had lain there for a very long time.

His mind was in turmoil. Should he set off back to camp and report it, or should he await the return of the foreman? That would be hours yet.

Unable to explain, even to himself, exactly why, he decided that he would stay and finish digging the hole.

This meant he would have to remove the corpse.

Meticulously Paddy worked to clear the peat from around the man. Finally uncovering him, Paddy saw that he was wrapped in some sort of cloak. Before long the whole body was free of the earth and gently Paddy pulled away the cloth covering his face.

A layer of peat had crept in under the fabric and this now masked his features.

Paddy felt as though he was in a dream.

Time had stopped making sense.

Here he was on a lovely summer's day, deep within a hole and looking into the face of a man who had drawn his last breath centuries before.

Why had he disturbed the body?

Why had he not reported it straight away?

How could he now explain his actions to that accursed foreman?

Having done one foolish thing, he now did another.

He stooped down, and putting his arms around the corpse he dragged it clear of the hole, laying him on the grass beside his sword.

Once clear he set to with a will, digging through the peat until after an hour or so of strenuous work his shovel finally hit the layer of hard gravel six foot down. Neatly, he finished the job as he had been ordered and carefully stowed the tools. The task set by the foreman was complete.

It was still only midday and the foreman was not expected back for at least a couple more hours.

What would he say about the body?

Paddy was tired and thirsty, and his thoughts strayed from the peaty corpse to one of a cool pint of beer.

Ah! But wouldn't that be grand.

On reflection, he recalled that the nearest public house was at least ten miles away. A great pity. But still, he had a drop of tea in his flask and a sandwich, and it was time for a bite to eat, was it not?

It felt strange to be sitting there, drinking tea in the company of the ancient body, but then what could be done about that? Thinking on this he ate up his sandwich and then taking his piece-box he filled it with the soft water from one of the many pools dotted around this rain-soaked, boggy landscape.

With some of the damp, soft moss, he began to sponge away the mess of liquid peat from the face. The visage of a young man emerged from Paddy's ministrations; a young man of possibly twenty years of age and, apart from a lump on his forehead, a perfect face.

'Holy Mother!' Paddy whispered, crossing himself, 'He could be sleeping.'

The sun disappeared behind a mass of clouds. A mist flowed down from the hill. That earlier feeling of dread hit Paddy with ever more force. A deep chill, like the ice cold steel of a sword, ran through him.

'I'll go and meet the boss,' he muttered to himself.

As he stumbled away in a state of mounting anxiety it crossed his mind to hide the sword.

No. He would not.

He left it lying beside its owner.

So, in the swirling mistiness, he set off down the rough path in the direction of the camp. The mist, which earlier had been merely a haze, was now a thick enveloping fog. It felt good though, to be on the move, to be heading back to his own world, away from the young man and his sword.

He strode on, ever more determined to put as

much distance as possible between himself and the strangeness born out of the peat bog.

Taking the wrong direction altogether – a mistake he realised rather too late – he stepped out over a cliff edge and plunged fifty feet or more to the rocky riverbed, whereupon his hard skull was split open upon a jutting rock.

The quiet, burbling river gently lifted and swept his lifeless form a short way downstream, before hiding him forever in a hole between two black boulders.

THE FOREMAN

It was normal at the roadworks for the foreman to make a thorough pest of himself; flying about as he did in the Land Rover; stopping off at various points to shout encouragement – more commonly perceived as threats; urging them on to ever greater efforts; and even sometimes being forced out of his Land Rover in sheer exasperation in order to show these men just how to swing a pick, or how to dig to greater advantage.

Were they feigning their ignorance?

The Foreman was a man too full of contempt to give any kind of credit to others, or indeed see any shortcomings within himself.

They were just plain ignorant, he thought to himself, feeling much ill-used and put upon.

Moreover, on this particular day, having returned from taking Paddy up the hill to the plain, he was also feeling a wee bit off-colour – not entirely surprising, winked the men, considering what he had put away in the village pub the night before – and so he thought that, as the resident engineer had gone home for the long weekend, he might put his feet up in the caravan for ten minutes or so.

Hours later he awoke.

Struggling to his feet he rubbed the sleep out of his eyes and, looking at his pocket watch, was horrified to see that it was nearly five o'clock and he still had to go and fetch that 'slacker'. Leaping into the Land Rover he shot back up the hill. The mist had cleared. Up and up he went. He felt sure that he would have met Paddy on the way; after all the hole should have been finished hours ago and he certainly wasn't back at the camp.

'Bloody, lazy, feckless skiver!' he fumed, inwardly imagining Paddy lying fast asleep in the sun when he should be back at work.

Arriving at the site there was no sign of Paddy. His tools were there, and the ranging rod was propped up in the centre of the very neatly dug hole.

He looked around.

Everything was in order.

To give him his due – which was an alien concept to the foreman – Paddy had made a tidy job of it before he left.

The foreman, though, was not in the least concerned about his missing workman. He was well used to, what he considered to be, these unpredictable Irishmen – here today, gone tomorrow.

So, gathering up the pick and shovel he chucked them into the back of the Land Rover and hurriedly drove back in time to let his weary men knock off at day's end, and get started on his own evening.

GUNN 1746

Gunn was his name. Oh, yes, he was as keen as any other of the young men in his village to fight for the Prince, but the horror of Culloden was something far beyond their youthful imaginations.

What chance had they had, he thought, tired and famished as they were. What chance against those men of Cumberland's, well-fed and well-armed as they were.

He had done his best, had he not.

He had thrown himself into that mad last-ditch charge at the enemy rifle fire, but to see his friends falling and screaming for their mothers and then dying all about him, well, the fear of death thrust itself deeply into his heart and could not be ignored.

He ran.

He felt a stab of shame as he seized his chance to slip away, unobserved, from the carnage of that bloody field; and he suffered a deep anguish at his own cowardice in hiding out amongst the thorns, watching as the murderous soldiers dispatched the wounded Highlanders with sword and bayonet.

No mercy shown.

He had lain there until darkness had fallen and then, with only a single thought in mind – that of home – he began the long trek West towards the village from whence he came. The going had been hard and along the way he had been reduced to begging for food from the kindly, but wary, crofter folk, themselves hungry – and scared too – at the thought of Cumberland's revenge on any who may offer alms to the enemy.

Sleeping on the rough moors and wrapped only in his long cloak, each hard mile covered brought him nearer to his home.

What would he find there?

At this thought his stomach lurched; what may

have happened to his family? Not all the people supported the Pretender's cause.

I cannot be thinking of that now, he thought, I will face that once I reach home. One more day should see me there. Oh, to see the faces of my mother and father once more, and my brothers and sisters. Never again will I leave.

In the distance his eyes caught sight of movement. A few cows were being driven to the high grassy plain, and as he got closer Gunn could see the drover. He recognised him – he was a fellow of his own age, a MacDonald, and a tormentor if ever there was one. An outspoken opponent of the rising. He realised, with dread, that the news of the disaster at Culloden would have travelled fast.

It had indeed.

'So here ye are, Gunn, running back home with your yellow tail between your legs. Not much good did you do at Culloden, eh! Running like a rabbit, are ye!'

The fact that there was more than a nugget of truth in MacDonald's scorn only increased Gunn's fury and he at once unsheathed his sword, but, quicker than a flash MacDonald picked up a stone and flung it at Gunn, hitting him squarely on the forehead. Gunn was felled instantly, his sword dropping from his already dead hand.

Whatever MacDonald's faults were he would never have betrayed Gunn to Cumberland's soldiers, and whatever their difference of view there had been no intent in his killing of the boy – a boy whom he had known since their childhood.

But although he was wracked with guilt, a need to preserve himself was uppermost in his mind.

Nobody must hear of this, he thought.

With the help of Gunn's own sword he cut and hacked into the peat and, clawing out the wet earth with his bare hands, he slowly dug a shallow grave.

Dragging Gunn's body into it he laid him out and as he gently covered the young face – one that he knew so well – with the cloak, and placed his sword upon the body, he uttered some words in prayer before kicking in the cold buttery peat and tamping it down with his feet.

GUNN 1998

We shall never know what aroused Gunn from his long sleep; he himself was unaware that he had slept at all, indeed he was conscious only that his head throbbed with pain and that his eyes could not focus properly. After a while, he took in the state of his cloak, clarted as it was in slimy peat. He could not understand what had befallen him – his head was fit to burst. Struggling to his feet, memories of his encounter with MacDonald loomed.

'That dog! He did this!'

He could see in his mind's eye MacDonald reaching for the stone and then... nothing.

His fingers felt tentatively at the hard lump on his forehead.

'He will pay for this!'

Gunn picked up his sword and rather shakily scraped the worst of the muck from his cloak with the sharp edge.

'My, God!' he exclaimed, 'I look as though I have been buried alive!'

Images of that vile MacDonald boy filled his head and with his words echoing in his mind – words full of filthy sarcasm and implications of cowardice – he vowed to have his revenge.

Looking around, he saw no sign of MacDonald.

Nothing moved on the face of the land. Even the cows had disappeared.

His eyes alighted on the deep pit with the painted pole in the middle and he puzzled over it for a brief moment.

Everything seemed strange today.

His head cleared, and with a new clarity of mind he swore to avenge the insult to himself. Sword in hand and revenge in his heart, he headed towards MacDonald's croft.

Tonight there would be a settlement.

THE MACDONALD CROFTHOUSE MUSEUM 1998

The Museum committee agreed to restore the ruin of the MacDonald's crofthouse to that which it had been way back in time – to a time even before the Clearances, when the native people, including the croft's last occupants, had been driven from their land and their homes to make way for sheep.

It was a novel idea.

There was a lot to do; the original walls were still there, although in a sorry state, and these were repaired; and the roof, which of course, had long gone, was thatched once more.

The hearth was placed at the centre of the house, a hole in the roof drew the smoke up and out – that is, when it was not swirling thickly around the small, dark interior.

It is hard to imagine living in such a house in these modern times, but it was authentic to that time past, and would be of great interest to visitors.

Indeed, many people came to visit the little Crofthouse Museum, especially those MacDonalds from faraway places such as America.

They were all made welcome as the museum committee was anxious for such people to savour the atmosphere of the old place – these people being the museum fund's most generous contributors.

Many strange questions and comments were made to the young curator, but he was quite taken aback when a young man from America announced that it was his own ancestors who had been the last inhabitants of the old crofthouse.

The young man was a MacDonald of course, and was delighted by the museum. He congratulated the curator and announced that it would give him great pleasure to make a handsome donation to the project. The chairman was summoned in order to receive a cheque for one thousand pounds, which he did, most gratefully. Following the presentation of the cheque young MacDonald came up with a most unusual request.

'What would you good folks say if I asked to spend the night alone in the old crofthouse?'

The chairman and the members of the committee looked at each other in surprise.

'So that I could really soak up the spirits of my ancestors!' he said, with a most appealing smile.

'Well...' the chairman hesitated.

'Hey, guys,' said the young American, 'I'm not looking for free accommodation or anything. What say I write you out another little cheque!'

'A splendid idea!' exclaimed the chairman, 'We will do everything we can to make it a unique experience for you, Mr. MacDonald! Would tomorrow night suit yourself?'

There was no doubt that the chairman and the curator went all out to make this a night to remember for the young man.

They prepared the old crofthouse as best they could. Tallow candles were brought in, a simple platter of bread and cheese was laid out and the peat fire was coaxed into life in the hearth, with the ensuing billowing clouds of smoke freely allowed to make their way out of whichever place they could find an exit – that occasionally being the chimney hole itself.

Truly, an authentic experience was created.

Young Mr. MacDonald was enchanted, even more so when presented with an outfit of typical crofter's clothes from those bygone days.

Suitably attired he took up occupation the next evening; everything was as it would have been two hundred years before.

He settled in and lit the candles. For even though it was still daylight outside and would be for hours yet – it being a summer evening in the northern hemisphere – inside the little crofthouse, with its tiny windows, it was as dark as night.

Warm and snug it was though, and quite comfortable once you got used to the smoke, so before very long the young man found himself yawning. Contentedly he lay back on the old wooden settle, absorbing through every pore as he did so, the spirits of his ancient ancestors.

Before long he fell into a deep sleep.

Gunn knew every step of the way to MacDonald's croft, and yet he was having some difficulty. The night had finally closed in, and in that summer darkness the landscape seemed slightly strange to his eyes. Over where he knew the village to be, bright lights were burning, some atop long poles.

He hadn't time to think of this right now.

He had an appointment to keep.

Blinking to clear his vision he eventually made out the outline of MacDonald's crofthouse and he saw a flicker of light emanating from the little window. He crept closer, and on peering in he could see the figure of MacDonald himself reclining on the settle.

'Got you, you swine!' he whispered, making ready with his sword.

MacDonald awoke to the crash of the old door being kicked violently in, and there in the dim light he observed a devilish figure brandishing a sword. For an instant, he thought that he was in a dream, but then it dawned upon him where he was and his face broke into a smile.

'My God, these museum guys are sure going out of their way to make things realistic!'

He was still smiling when Gunn's sword passed through his windpipe before embedding its sharp point deeply into the wood of the old settle.

There the young MacDonald was found when at 9 a.m. prompt, the curator came to ensure that the crofthouse was fit to receive another flood of visitors.

The roiling inner rage ebbed away from Gunn, leaving him exhausted and spent. It was replaced by a sense of the hopelessness of his situation.

Not that he felt remorse for his violent and brutal dispatch of MacDonald.

That he did not.

But he was now a murderer and as such he would be hunted down by the young man's family.

And as a soldier who had fought for Charlie's cause he would be hunted down by Cumberland's men.

And as a deserter... well...

One way or another his life was over.

In the dim, flickering light, he looked down at his clothes and his body, still filthy from the peat bog despite all his efforts to clean them.

Taking one last look at the object of his rage, lying skewered to the settle with his sword, he retreated out of the crofthouse into the fresh air of the summer night.

He remembered the cave where, as children, they had played. He would hide there, at least for a while.

As dawn approached he found his way easily to the little burn. There beside a shallow pool he stripped himself of his foul clothes, and kneeling in the sparkling water he washed himself, scrubbing at his peat-stained skin with rough grass and the soft, damp moss; then lying back in the sweet flowing stream, still warm from the sun of the long summer days, he let the gentle silken waters run over his body.

He felt, at last, a sense of calm.

He was cleansed, purified and at peace.

The last remaining traces of the preserving peat washed away. The water gently dispersed the dirt, and the filth, and then his skin and his very flesh. The soft components of Gunn's body – reduced to fatty foam – hurried seaward in the burbling water.

Soon, after Gunn's empty skull had rolled and tumbled away downstream with the insistent water, all that remained in the shallow pool was a collection of bones.

THE FOREMAN

News of the brutal murder of the young American made headlines around the world. Calls from home and abroad, and from strangers from every nook and cranny of the globe flooded in, demanding that the perpetrator be caught.

Roadblocks were set up and watchful officers of the law were stationed at all air and ferry ports.

At the roadworks, the foreman was the centre of attention for the umpteenth time.

Never short of a damning word, he now took righteous pleasure in uttering to the wide world:

'I never did trust that bloody Irishman!'

The Baas

....

During the war, when herring fishing was resumed at Ullapool, there were lean times, but also periods of plenty as is ever the case with herring fishing.

In times of plenty, drifters came in loaded to the gunwales with the *silver darlings*, but much of the fish sadly went to waste for the simple reason that transport, to take the fish to market, was difficult to organise in wartime. Because of this situation somebody decided to bring in a ship on which the surplus catch could be rendered into meal.

The vessel was Norwegian and she was called "The Baas". I suppose she must have been one of the first klondykers to arrive in our waters. She lay at anchor in the village bay and – unfortunately – whenever the wind was blowing from the south, she absolutely stank the place out.

Oh, a hellish smell, it must be said.

147

Anyway, Willie Chalan worked at Rhidorroch for Colonel Rose, only coming home to his house in Pulteney Street at weekends. He lived where John Campbell and his sisters live now. The house then was not the spick and span place that it is now, but was quite adequate nonetheless.

I suppose one might also say that Willie Chalan was not the brightest person one had ever met, but he was a hard-working and regular type of man – even though he took a good dram at the weekend.

He was the one who enquired, after a furious fist fight outside the Caley Bar with another equally inebriated local:

'How many black eyes have I?'

And was quite happy to hear, 'Only two!'

However, this was by and by.

Willie Chalan came home on his bike from Rhidorroch after a week of hard graft and, as usual, went to the butcher's and bought a nice piece of beef which would do for the weekend and maybe would last him into the coming week. Indeed, it was a good lump of meat and so he put it away in the larder until he was ready to cook it.

After a week away from home there were plenty of tasks to be done around the house and these he attended to with quiet contentment. It was whilst he was in and out of the house that he first noticed a rather unpleasant smell.

At first he thought nothing of it; Ullapool, with its cows, byres, hens, and middens and the like, never mind the outhouses, was a rather more rural and earthy place than it is now, and so consequently various strange odours would waft their ways up, down and around the streets, making their way into the houses and under the noses of every villager alike.

It showed no favour to one nor the other.

And so this awful odour had found its way into Willie's house and Willie's nose.

This terrible smell began to worry Willie Chalan.

It seemed to be becoming more and more pungent and Willie, being basically a clean person, searched through his house in fear that a rat may have died in some dark corner, but he could find nothing amiss.

Then it struck him – the meat must have gone off! Admittedly the weather was warm, but damn it all he had only just bought it!

In a rage he took the "offending" meat, dug a hole in the back garden and flung it in, angrily throwing the earth back in over it and, for good measure, stamping on it angrily with his big boots.

That devil of a butcher, he thought indignantly.

It was too late in the day to go back to the butcher's and complain and, anyway, he had no more ration coupons with which to get more.

In a rather disgusted mood he fed his dog on some scraps and set off for the bar at the Caley.

It was just as he was passing the bank that somebody shouted over in greeting and remarked on the horrible stench coming from that bloody ship!

The Baas!

That was what it was.

Willie Chalan stopped as if struck by a bullet and whirling around he made tracks back to his house at his best speed.

He rushed to the shed to fetch his spade and proceeded, with haste, to dig up the weekend meat, but alas, too late – his trusted dog had beaten him to it.

This *trusty* dog was now looking up into his Master's face rather sheepishly, and on realising that his Master could indeed see him (having failed to render himself invisible) and was looking at him with a murderous expression, he looked away ashamedly, whilst surreptitiously licking his blood-spattered chops.

Poor Willie, his Sunday dinner was now going to be a rather spartan affair.

The Birdman of Braemore

Robbie Sawyer, as his name suggests, was a woodsman in the proper sense of the word. He was an expert in every aspect of his trade, coming as he did from a long line of sawyers – woodsmen for generations and generations.

Although he was still connected to the family business, he had broken away and now chose to conduct his own affairs as a consultant in timber works and, due to his knowledge, his advice was respected and much sought after.

When Morris Shipman received a contract to build an upmarket yacht in good class timber, he was advised to get Robbie Sawyer to source the best larch for the planking, and oak for the heavier frames. Robbie gave him some helpful advice and offered to point out the required trees, still growing in the forest, and even to fell them; he could also arrange the machining of the fallen trees, to the exact dimensions required by the builder, and this all could be done at his father's sawmill in Inverness-shire.

Most satisfactory, thought Morris.

And so, at a later date, the boat builder came to view the standing timber, as Robbie had suggested, and here they now were, together, trundling up the rough track to the woodland wherein the chosen trees were growing.

'Here we are, Mr. Shipman,' announced Robbie, slowing the rough old Land Rover to a stop at the end of the track to the plantation.

Here were the trees. Morris was entranced.

Never before had he come to view his building material, never mind material that was still growing in the warm earth.

Robbie was in his element, these mighty trees were his world and he was eager to share his interest and knowledge of the wild place with this man, a man who seldom moved from his own very different element – the sea.

'That's your boat standing there,' joked the young woodsman pointing out a great larch rising up tall and straight, then turning, he indicated the larch's neighbour, an ancient oak, 'And there is the good old oak to hold her all together.'

The boat builder was much impressed by these mighty and ancient trees, reaching skywards in their glory. He knew that the timber offered was exactly what he required and that Robbie was the very man to organise the processing of the wood, and so an agreement was reached on an honest handshake.

Of course, Robbie knew this countryside well,

but even he had failed to notice that, high above the trees on the craggy skyline, was a raven's nest, from where, with glittering eyes, the scene below was being witnessed with something less than enthusiasm – indeed alarm.

The birds cawed stridently to the trees below, asking firstly the larch, 'What do you think, brother Larch, now that you will be cut down and made into a boat?'

The foolish larch answered excitedly, 'Did you not hear? I'm not just going to be an ordinary boat. I'm going to be a big beautiful yacht! One cannot wish for better than that.'

A rough gravelly voice intervened. It was the old oak, also aware of his imminent fate at the hands of the executioner, Robbie Sawyer. In his time he had witnessed the felling of many old friends by this man and his dreadful chainsaw.

The old oak angrily growled to the larch, 'Thou fool, do you not know that for a hundred years I've protected you from the easterly wind, winter and summer, from the time you were a tiny sapling. Now you stand a hundred feet tall and straight as a die – all thanks to me!'

The larch said nothing, so the old oak, feeling his sap rise up in indignation, added, 'Are you now prepared to sacrifice yourself – and me – so that some bodger can turn you into a fancy boat? No, it must not happen!'

High above the larch and the oak the ravens heard the discordant voices of the trees and crawed down suggesting that they would be pleased to disrupt the efforts of those greedy human ants.

With their clever brains and dark magical powers

they, as ravens, might be able to put a stop to this vandalism of their precious woodland world.

It was quite true that the oak had sheltered the larch, with the result that the now tall larch, if anything, had inclined slightly towards the oak. On felling, the larch would topple and drop into the arms of the ancient oak, thereby causing damage to both. This was a problem that Robbie Sawyer was well aware of – it would need to be carefully rigged so that this would not happen.

Morris Shipman was excited about his new adventure and urged Robbie to press ahead as soon as possible. They discussed the felling angle and Morris shared his own experiences with rigging and high masts.

It was decided.

The larch would come down first.

They would rig the tree there and then, in preparation for felling the following day.

Agile as a monkey, Robbie climbed the towering larch with the end of the rigging rope around his waist. Higher and higher he rose, leaving Morris below paying out the strong nylon rope. When he was high enough, he shouted down that work could begin on the rigging plan they had agreed upon.

Firstly, the lower end of the rope was to pass through the pulley block he had affixed to an adjoining tree – this would give them the correct felling angle; the free end of the rope would then be put around the tow bar of the Land Rover which, before the first slice was cut into the tree, would be backed up, pulling and straining the tree to one side, and thus allowing the great tree to fall clear of the mighty old oak.

But all that was for tomorrow, Robbie thought, and securely made his end fast to the tree trunk – sixty feet above the ground.

He loved being up here and, standing as he was on a high branch and looking around at this landscape, he was loath to ever come down. He knew it so well from the ground, but from up here it was like entering a new world.

He felt at one with the birds.

This new world spread out from the trees below, extending out to the sharp edge of the far-off horizon.

Looking towards the skyline of the high cliff he saw for the first time the ravens' ancient nesting area. These were nests that were built on, again and again, being passed down through the generations by the ravens who had come before.

A precious place indeed.

But now thunderclouds were gathering in.

Looking at their black forms rolling heavily in like a tidal wave, Robbie said to himself, 'Oh! Bad omen!'

At the very instant a bolt of lightning struck the top of the larch tree – the violence of which threw the woodsman clean off his lofty perch.

The boat builder, almost blinded by the lightning flash, watched in disbelief. He saw his friend being flung from the tree. His fall seemed to take forever – he would most certainly be fatally injured when he landed. And land he eventually did.

Rushing over to the now grounded man, he was astonished to see him attempting to rise – indeed within a second, less even, he had attained a kneeling posture – and here he was now, half standing and flapping his arms around. Piteous, croaking sounds were emanating from deep within his throat – he sounded almost like a wounded bird.

Morris knew that Robbie required medical help – and soon. He radioed for help. But, in this very remote place, the boat builder was not able to give their exact location, and so it took a long while and numerous attempts before the ambulance finally arrived at the scene.

Robbie was still crowing and flapping.

'He's in a bad way,' said Morris.

The ambulance lads agreed and, quickly loading the injured man into the vehicle, they made speed for the hospital in Inverness, with Morris vainly trying to keep up in Robbie's old Land Rover.

Let us now return to the forest where the shocking accident occurred.

There stood the two trees.

The ancient oak was peaceful and still, and now snoozing in the light breeze, and there, the stately larch was still standing tall, but was swaying and sighing – in mourning for the loss of his dream of being transformed into a beautiful yacht, and escaping this forest to sail the world over.

On the high cliff, the ravens were exultant in their victory – cawing throatily and boastfully to one another, 'We are the champions!'

'Those dumb trees down there owe their lives to us!' they cawed triumphantly.

Obviously, after being struck by lightning and falling sixty feet or more from the tree, Robbie was lucky to be alive, and at the hospital it was agreed that his physical condition was remarkably good considering the fall. It was thought that – given time – he would regain his normal voice and physical fitness, and so eventually he was released and he returned to his woodland caravan.

Morris Shipman too suffered from the accident – he was shocked, albeit in a different way to Robbie. He wondered if he was entirely in his comfort zone with regard to building wooden boats, and when he went to visit Robbie he confessed, sadly, that he was no longer interested in the project. Robbie, in his still croaked, creaky voice answered in agreement, indicating – his head strangely bobbing up and down – that he too wanted to change his life, further frightening the still nervous Morris by hopping up onto the end of the bed, flapping his arms and cawing and pecking at the blankets.

Oh...he's still not himself at all! thought Morris, backing quickly out of the caravan door.

News of these events had winged their way through the entire raven community and in the higher echelons of that strict sect there was a certain amount of disquiet – had the local branch of ravens used their powers irresponsibly?

Certainly, a meeting at the local level must be called and action should be taken if necessary. Indeed, the Head of Highland Ravens himself would have to be in attendance.

A date was set aside for the hearing.

On the day, interested ravens jetted in from near and far. The whole matter was gone over and statements were made by all ravens involved. All were listened to intently by the old Head of Highland Ravens, who, speaking in his immaculate "*higher ravenese*", stated that he was satisfied that no permanent or damaging effects had been suffered, and he brought the meeting to a close with a loud hammer of his mighty beak on the tree trunk.

Justice had been done, and the judgement echoed throughout the forest giving rise to much rejoicing and hearty congratulations all around.

The ancient oak soughed gently in the breeze, while the larch moaned sadly, both still firmly rooted amongst their many old neighbours.

The ravens returned to their nests and to their hungry young – a new generation of guardians for the wood had been born.

About a month later the ravens on the high cliff noted Robbie Sawyer's Land Rover driving into the woodland. Keeping quiet they worriedly watched the man climbing the great larch.

Ah! Thankfully, all he had come to do was unfasten and retrieve his rope, after which he made off down the track, hopping from time to time and humming an old Scots tune – "Oh, Rowan Tree":

> Oh rowan tree, oh rowan tree
> > Thou'lt aya be dear to thee
> Entwined thou art wi' many ties
> > O'hame and infancy
> Thy leaves were aye the first of spring
> > Thy flowers the summer's pride
> There was nae sic a bonnie tree
> > In a' the country side
> Oh rowan tree

As all who heard agreed, he had quite a nice voice *for a human* and – with him not waving his arms around anymore, nor yet pecking – they settled back on their branches and raucously joined him in his song.

Life in the forest had sweetly resumed.

The Egg Poacher

....

Sadly, old Donald Macgregor passed away leaving his croft, on the heights of Braes, in the care of a few sheep, a flock of hens, his grieving widow, Marie, but most importantly his dog.

The dog was a young and very vigorous animal and had doted upon his master – a devotion that his master shared and returned – and so he was puzzled that Donald had taken off without a word.

Never mind, he was a dog of strong character, and whilst his master was away he would assume command.

Meanwhile, down below in the village of Ullapool there was a mother instructing her young son to journey up to the Macgregor's croft to get the dozen eggs that had been promised her by Marie.

This was a regular event. He had been up there many times before. But it would feel a bit strange, he thought to himself, now that Mr. Macgregor had gone '*to his reward*', as his mother had told him. What might the reward be, he found himself wondering, as he dawdled along on this balmy spring day.

He certainly knew what he would like – a boat with a fine pair of oars

Or maybe one with an engine?

He had no idea at all what Mr. Macgregor might choose as he wasn't really acquainted with him, himself always being away at the sheep with that awful fierce dog.

Oh, he thought, stopping dead in his tracks – *that awful fierce dog*!

He may be at home!

For a moment his young mind was filled with dread, but, on second thoughts, maybe the dog would have gone to his reward too. After all Mr. Macgregor's reward would surely be incomplete without his dog.

Of course!

This made complete sense and his young mind, freed from anxiety, returned to visions of his future and the receiving of his own reward, and he continued on, wending his way up the steep hill, now clothed in sweet-smelling broom.

Eventually the boy arrived at the croft. Marie had told his mother that he should just go in, and that he would find the bag of eggs on the table, and so he entered the blossoming croft garden and plodded upwards to the little white house. Thankfully, there was no sign of the dog lying in wait and so he opened the door and peeped in and there indeed were the eggs over on the table.

He called out timidly, 'Hello?'

All was silent.

Sighing with relief he darted over, reaching out for the eggs.

'Grrr!'

Whirling around he snatched his hand back and watched in terror as the dog, growling and circling around him, finally took up a post at the doorway, thereby cutting off the boy's only route of escape. The dog's lips were drawn up and back, and all that could be seen were a mouthful of big, sharp, salivating, canine teeth. This was not a smile, certainly not in doggy terms.

The dog had his own view of the scene unfolding before him.

Here was some little urchin from down there below the hill – that foreign land full of poachers and ne'er do wells. Hah! He had always known that these people needed watching, and now he had caught one in the very act of stealing from his beloved master and mistress.

It was an outrage.

The fact that he had let his guard down, allowing the boy to sneak into the house was a little humiliating, and he was now regretting having had that little nap. But the warmth from the shaft of sunlight streaming through the window, and the steady tick tock of the clock had unfortunately overpowered him.

He felt shame.

His master had been away for a long while – where could he be? – and had he known of this lapse, he would not be pleased. But wherever he may be, the dog resolved to do his duty and guard this house, and his mistress, until his master's return.

So there we have it.

A stand off between boy and dog.

After a time in the balmy heat of the kitchen both beings softened like candle-wax. The dog slumped in front of the door, his eyelids slowly drooping. The imprisoned boy, although fearful to take his eyes off the dog, could not stifle a yawn and he too melted drowsily into a seat by the table where he began to whistle softly.

It was a tune he knew well and one that he thought the dog might like.

But the dog did *not*.

Indeed, his round bright eyes flicked open and with a low growl he stopped the racket instantly. The boy was the kind of boy though, that could not be silent for long, and soon the room was filled with the soft hum of a gaelic air that his mother had taught him, and that he was going to perform at the coming annual Mòd.

The dog's eyes flicked open once again, but this time he looked at the boy with something amounting to appreciation. The boy, emboldened, decided to try out his song on the dog:

> *Ho ró mo nighean donn bhòidheach,*
> > *Hi rì mo nighean donn bhòidheach,*
> *Mo chaileag, laghach, bhòidheach,*
> > *Cha phòsainn ach thu.*
>
> *A pheigi donn nam blàth-shùl,*
> > *Gur trom a thug mi gràdh dhuit;*
> *Tha t'iomhaigh, ghaoil, 'us t'ailleachd*
> > *A ghnàth tigh'nn fo'm'ùidh.*

Ho ro my nut-brown maiden,
    Hi ri my nut-brown maiden,
Ho ro ro maiden,
    For she's the maid for me.

Her eye so mildly beaming,
    Her look so frank and free,
In waking or in dreaming,
    Is evermore with me.

The dog arose, his ears perked up and tilting his head inquisitively to one side he looked at the boy with an altogether more gentle regard. The prisoner wondered what was in the dog's mind. What should he do? Should he make a mad dash for the door?

But what about the eggs?

No. He couldn't leave without the eggs.

However, the atmosphere in the croft had greatly softened. There was a warmth that was due, not just to the golden shafts of sunlight filling the wee kitchen and sparkling off the copper pans, but rather to a growing and mutual understanding between these two beings.

Maybe, thought the dog, this urchin was not such a devil of an egg poacher after all.

Maybe, thought the boy, this dog was not the evil beast of Hades that he had imagined him to be.

The dog slowly padded over to the boy and placed his muzzle upon the boy's knees. The boy's hand could not but help reach down and stroke the warm silken head that had been so gently offered to him.

They looked intently into each others eyes and saw neither anger, nor fear.

The dog whined softly along as the boy sang the

gentle gaelic air, a song that the dog had heard his master sing many times before.

The bang of the door as it swung open broke up this dreamy scene. It was Marie with her meagre weeks shopping, hot and tired out from the climb back up the road from Ullapool.

'Is this you, still here?' she said in surprise.

The boy, regaining his poise, replied that it was indeed himself, but that the dog had insisted that he stay.

'We have become great friends,' said the boy as the excited dog jumped up and licked his face.

Marie was pleased, the dog had been so *gruamach* since Donald's passing.

'How do you explain such a thing to an animal?'

It made her happy to see him bouncing around once more.

'Come back and see us soon,' said Marie with a smile, an invitation that was echoed by an excited bark from the dog.

As the boy happily wandered back down the hill with the eggs, he revisited what he would like for his reward at life's end.

A boat with a fine pair of oars.

Or maybe one with an engine?

And yes, just such a dog.

Through the Storm

....

Some old photographs, showing many distressed fishing vessels blown off their moorings and driven ashore around Lochbroom, have recently emerged. One glance at these prints was enough to remind me of my younger self in that winter of 1953 when this event occurred.

I was involved in quite a painful way with this, perhaps, worst storm of my life.

Not on a boat, nor yet a ship, but unbelievably on a darn motorbike.

Let me tell you about it.

I had just completed my apprenticeship in engineering at the shipyard of Wm. Denny of Dumbarton and had signed up to sail on one of Shaw Saville's liners bound for Australia and so had to come back to Ullapool to get rigged out for my new career at sea. But, before leaving these shores, I had to get rid of my motorbike which, despite advertising, had remained unsold. I would now have to take it back to Ullapool, or rather, it would take me, I thought.

The trip to Ullapool should be no problem and I was looking forward to a few weeks off before joining my ship. In short, I was excited about this new chapter in my life, and I hurriedly prepared my bike for the journey.

My friend, Hugh, was there in the darkness at 5 a.m. prompt on the day of departure to see me off, but he warned me that his father was forecasting bad weather, and, worried as he was by his father's words, he suggested that perhaps I should delay it.

'No way,' I said, and heedlessly kicked the engine into life, and with a sense of exaltation I powered away from my old life in Dumbarton.

Free at last.

Home first and then the rest of the world.

Although the wind was picking up Loch Lomond was passed in good order.

No traffic on the road at all.

Not a car.

Not a bike.

Where were they all?

I was very soon overtaken by another lone biker mounted on a fancy top-of-the-range Vincent Black Shadow no less and kitted out to the nth degree.

He roared on past despite the road showing ominous signs of a past shower of icy hail. I saw him again a few miles on, stopped now at the roadside, savouring a cup of coffee from his flask. I wondered if he would be heading on or beating a retreat, and enviously, I eyed the hot steam rising from his cup.

He eyed me back, shaking his head in disapproval

at this ill-clad figure trailing by.

I pressed on, even more ill-clad now that my hat had blown off and away across the heather.

A sleety wind was now playing hell with my luxuriant golden locks, and stinging and blinding my un-goggled eyes.

I reminded myself of my sunny future.

Crianlarich now behind me.

Hail and Rain.

Heading now for Ballachulish and the ferry.

The wind was now very strong and the road surface a quagmire of slush.

Sliding and slipping.

Glencoe was a nightmare, with fiendish squalls from all directions blowing my bike from one side of the road to the other, as if I'd been no more than a birch leaf.

What had I been thinking?

But still, at no point did I consider turning back.

I had burnt my boats and thankfully there were no other vehicles to collide with.

I was the only idiot out.

I reached the ferry at Ballachulish.

Not a living soul around.

I pounded at the door of the ferryman's shed. Eventually, the iron door creaked open a couple of inches and, through the roaring wind, I shouted into the figure cowering within, 'Is the ferry running?'

The only answer before the door crashed shut?

'Are you out of your bloody mind!'

I was now faced with an extra thirty miles around the head of the loch.

Freezing, wet and miserable I headed now for Drumnadrochit. I would have to bypass Inverness for legal reasons (road tax etc.) and this meant that I would have to tackle the hill road to Beauly.

Madness.

The surface was thickly coated with ice.

The temperature was getting lower and, what with the wind and the treacherous armour coating of ice on the road, it became impossible to stay on the bike.

To reach the top of the hill I would have to get off and walk. With the engine running and in low gear I matched the throttle to my sluggish, exhausted, walking pace.

What a slog.

My misery being further heaped upon by squalls of blattering hail.

Garve now.

Nearly home, I thought.

But no, worse was to come.

Heavy snow had fallen. The few vehicles that had passed had ploughed the snow into, now frozen, deep furrows.

More unintentional dismounting.

My falls, at least, were cushioned by the crusty snow.

So cold now.

My hands frozen with my fingers like claws.

Praise God! Loch Broom ahead.

The temperature rising at last and the blessed sea in sight.

But what a sight I saw before me.

The loch was reasonably calm, but nearly every beach was covered by cast-ashore fishing boats.

What could possibly have happened?

I didn't stop – home was too close now and I felt my mother beckoning me on. Arriving at Ullapool in the late afternoon, I was overjoyed to see her, just as she was setting off to feed the hens.

I was truly home now.

Was it worth the pain?

Yes, it was.

Did I ever get back on a motorbike again?

No, I did not.

A BRIEF ADDENDUM

On the night of January 31st through until the morning of February 1st, 1953, violent storms swept right across Scotland, England, Belgium and the Netherlands. A high spring tide combined with a severe European windstorm over the North Sea caused a storm tide. The combination of wind, high tide, and low pressure led to a water level of more than 18 feet above mean sea level in some places.

Hundreds of people died on that terrible night.

This was the reason for that sorry sight I had come across – the fishing fleet washed up at Leckmelm.

Thankfully, their crews had been on weekend leave and were safe at home on the east coast ports they hailed from – Peterhead, Banff, Lossiemouth, Buckie, and other such places. Only two of the boats suffered serious damage and in the following days and weeks all were recovered. Together, the crewmen of the boats formed a large workforce, salvaging one boat at a time, until the boats were once more afloat and the beaches were clear.

The people of the locality provided food and meals for these hard-working men, their efforts being coordinated by Captain Cooper, of 'the Captain's Cabin' fame (an Ullapool institution), who was later honoured for his efforts on behalf of the hard-wrought fishermen, and while the beaching of the boats at Loch Broom was a disaster for the fishermen, at least there were no injuries or fatalities.

One of the worst tragedies of that night was the loss of the M.V. Princess Victoria (also built at Denny's shipyard) as she headed for Northern Ireland, captained by James Ferguson. She had left Stranraer's railway loading pier with 128 passengers and 51 crew, and was carrying 44 tons of cargo. Heavy seas breached her stern doors and, with tons of water flooding her car deck, she capsized.

There were only 44 survivors and notably none of the ship's officers were amongst them.

We should pause from time-to-time and think of those out at sea, and wish them all a safe passage home to their families and loved ones – theirs is a hard and often dangerous life.

The Old Pear Tree

....

Most of us older people remember the Old Pear Tree standing alongside Market Street, its branches bending under the heavy burden of fruit that she bore every summer, year in year out, for perhaps a century or more.

Alas, the ancient tree is now long gone.

But here is my tale:

It was evening; Mother and Father sat by the cosy fireside whilst the boy doodled away at his homework at the table, not progressing too well.

'Isn't it time you went for the milk?' said Mother, addressing her son.

Father raised his head from the book he was reading and fixing the boy with a piercing look, but without uttering one word, indicated that Mother's words should be acted upon without delay.

The boy shuffled slowly to his feet and picking up

the milk pail and struggling into his jacket, reluctantly left the warmth of the snug room, hastening out into the cold night air of early October, en route to Market Street where creamy fresh milk was to be had at Jeck's place, at the far end of the road.

It was dark outside, especially as no street lights were permitted in wartime, but the sky was clear and frosted with a million stars glittering up yonder, and the sight of the Milky Way recalled him to his mission.

It would not take long to get the milk and the boy swung the tin pail fully around as he marched along.

He liked that pail, it was so useful.

For instance, when passing the water pump with its lions head at the junction of Ladysmith Street and Market Street, he could half fill the pail with water and have a good long drink from it, rather than putting his mouth to the lips of the lion and getting very wet in the process.

Oh yes!

A pail had its uscs.

And what about centrifugal force?

The boy had discovered this phenomenon with the half-full pail.

By whirling it around he discovered that the pail still continued to hold the water, even when upside down and at the highest point of its rotation, high over his head.

Magic!

However, onwards to the next thing of interest.

The Pear Tree.

Pears were the boy's passion. He loved pears and that tree had thousands. It was said that the fruits growing from it in such profusion were as hard as rocks, but how did anyone know this? He for one did not believe that, but as far as the boy knew nobody had ever dared to pluck a pear from it.

With good reason.

This bounteous pear tree was growing in the Headmaster's garden. A man to be kept clear of at all costs, especially by school boys.

What a challenge, the boy thought to himself. Would I have the nerve to climb the tree?

Was he scared?

Yes, he was.

In spite of his fear, in the quietness of this starlit night and clutching the pail, he moved nearer to the trunk. The pail would be handy if he should just happen to find one or two falling from the lower branches – no such luck.

He knew then that, should he want to take a bit out of a sweet and juicy pear, he must actually climb the tree. From earlier observation in the daytime he had noted that the best pears were at the very top. The fruit up there, closest as it was to the sun, was ripening to a glorious, golden, honey-brown.

These were the ones to have.

Would he attempt to climb?

Yes, he would.

And putting his fears aside he jumped nimbly onto the wall. From there it was easy to get into the lower branches. Here he found the pail to be a hindrance to climbing, so he decided to leave it on top of the wall. He would have to content himself with filling his pockets full of the succulent fruit.

Skilfully he scaled the tree, but on nearing the top he hesitated – a woman's voice was issuing forth from the lighted window at the rear of the house.

'Donald, dear, if you are going to light that smelly pipe could you please get out of my kitchen!'

Then a feared, but very familiar, voice grunted grumpily back and the back door shunted open, allowing "Dear Donald" – puffing mightily on the polluting pipe – to enter the garden to enjoy the cold evening air.

He was, thankfully, at present unaware of the potential pear-pincher shivering high up in the tree, and he contented himself with pacing peacefully to and fro.

He is bound to see the milk pail, thought the boy, as the Headmaster dropped anchor right below him, puffing out a thick cloud of pungent smoke.

The boy stealthily moved to a more secure position, nearer to the trunk. It would not do to come crashing down through the slender branches and land at the feet of the dreaded Headmaster.

Or onto his head!

The outcome could not be imagined!

Six of the best at least!

What saved this foolish boy from a fate worse than death?

It is true that it was maybe not worse than death, but the Headmaster was known far and wide for his mighty arm and the boy trembled at the thought of the thick, leather strap thwacking down on his outstretched hand.

What saved him, was a sudden change in the weather.

A great black cloud sailed overhead.

No, not tobacco smoke – though that might have been what precipitated it.

No. Just a cloud. It drew a thick curtain over the

starry heavens and unleashed its cargo of rain.

Now it was not so pleasurable to be outside.

The Headmaster, with some regret, tamped down the burning embers in his pipe with his thumb, knocked the spent tobacco out on the stone wall, and weighing anchor, he made his way quickly to the back door, pleading with his wife to be allowed in.

'Please, my dear, the pipe is out, I assure you!'

In the increasing darkness of the night he had, thankfully, failed to see the incriminating milk pail only feet away from his normally gimlet eyes.

Hearing the kitchen door open, and then firmly close, meant that the Headmaster was back in dock for the night.

Boy, what a relief!

He could now make a leisurely descent from the tree – but before that… surely it was fitting to pick a few beauties, especially now that the black cloud had drifted away and he could clearly see his prey silhouetted against the heavens.

What could possibly go wrong?

All danger had passed, had it not?

'Just six of the best!' meaning pears not thwacks, he thought with glee.

These he gathered carefully, and finally making his descent he strolled the short way to Jeck's, where the pail was filled with delicious fresh milk.

Home at last and without a drop of milk spilt.

'Where on earth have you been?' asked his mother, 'What a time you have taken.'

Perhaps they understood when their son produced six lovely golden pears and on enquiring as to just where he might have found such bounty he replied:

'Oh, it's nothing, the ground is covered with them.'

As they sat together eating the sweet fruit, Mother and Father looked at each other with that look that suggested *boys will be boys*.

Don't Be Long

. . . .

The boy, Edward, lived with his mother – the boy's father having left the home some years earlier and strangely failing to return to his loving wife and child. What had happened to him was never discovered. However, mother and child lived happily together.

The mother, Elizabeth, kept the small dockside house in good order and looked after Teddy, as she called him, really well.

This morning, as Teddy was preparing to go to school, his mother said, 'Teddy dear, could you please run along to the bakers and get half a dozen rolls. And don't be long, for you must not be late for school.'

Dutifully, Teddy hurried out of the house heading for the baker's shop, which was also on the dockside. It was a busy location with traffic going to and fro to the ships tied up at the quay.

Teddy was very interested in these ships, perhaps wondering if his father had left on one of them, and stopping for a brief while he gazed down at a huge and beautiful clipper, fully laden.

There was the Bosun pacing about the deck.

Teddy called down, 'Are you getting ready to sail?'

Looking upwards, the Bosun saw this fine-looking young lad and shouted back heartily, 'Aye, just waiting for the tugs.'

'Where are you going, sir?' asked Teddy.

'Australia!' came the reply, and with a wink and a smile he added, 'Do you want to come too?'

'Can I?' asked Teddy, already climbing down onto the deeply loaded ship.

The crew was now emerging from the fo'c'sle to work on making the vessel ready to be towed out to sea. Hopefully, she would be favoured with the necessary winds that, in time, would drive her all the way to Australia, and bring her all the way back again.

To be fair to the Bosun, can I suggest that, what with the crew busily milling about the deck, and the fact that he himself being not altogether fit for work due to alcoholic indulgence from the previous night, well... maybe he could have overlooked the presence of young Teddy?

Teddy was now very *keen* to go to Australia and on this ship too.

So, unbeknownst to everyone, he hid away under the canvas covers of one of the ship's lifeboats.

From within the humid darkness, he could hear the crew shambling about under orders from the Bosun, and he heard the throb of the tugs' engines as they arrived to tow the great sailing ship out to sea. He could smell the smoke and hear the noise of their paddle wheels beating, and the shouting of orders. Finally, he felt the movement of the great vessel as she was warping away from the quay.

People called out from the shore, 'Fare thee well!' as she was towed down the river.

It was all very exciting to young Teddy.

Soon the great ship could taste the salty sea under her stem and feel the clean sea wavelets rippling along her sides. A faint breeze allowed the crew to loosen some canvas to speed up her progress to more open water, whereupon the smoky tugs could finally be dispensed with.

As the day passed the Master of the ship ordered the tugs off – now having sufficient sea room and a favourable wind. Ireland disappeared on his starboard quarter as he made sail.

With the noise of the thumping tug engines gone there came a wonderful silence. Teddy could hear the sea slapping the ship's sides, and the wind snapping at the sails, and over it all were the rousing cries and shanties from a now sober crew.

> *I'll sing you a song of the fish of the sea,*
>   *Way, Rio!*
> *I'll sing you a song of the fish of the sea,*
>   *And we're bound for the Rio Grande!*
>
> *Then away, love, away,*
>   *Way, Rio!*
> *So fare ye well, my pretty young gal,*
>   *We are bound for the Rio Grande!*

So man the good capstan and run it around,
  Way, Rio!
We'll heave up the anchor to this jolly sound,
  For we're bound for the Rio Grande!

Then away, love, away,
  Way, Rio!
So fare ye well, my pretty young gal,
  We are bound for the Rio Grande!

Our ship went a-sailing out over the bar,
  Way, Rio!
We pointed her nose for the southeren star,
  For we're bound for the Rio Grande!

Then away, love, away,
  Way, Rio!
So fare ye well, my pretty young gal,
  We are bound for the Rio Grande!

The anchor is weighed and the sails they are set,
  Way, Rio!
The maids that we're leaving we'll never forget,
  For we're bound for the Rio Grande!

He was filled with so many new emotions as he lay in hiding in the dark, listening to their rousing song. Scared, but excited, he emerged into the light, to the shock of all before him. The joyful shanty ended and he was roughly hustled aft to face the wrath of the captain, whereupon he was entered in the ship's log as a stowaway, and as such was put to work.

And work he did, under a hard Bosun who turned this callow schoolboy into a competent sailor man.

Three years on the great sailing ship again entered the muddy river and was towed up to the quay she had left thousands of sea miles before.

Teddy, now a hardened seaman, looked ashore at his home port.

Not a lot had changed there.

But he was home.

There were ships aplenty, some loading, others discharging. Sadly, there were fewer sailing ships than before and many more foul smoking steamers.

At last, the great clipper was warped alongside and made fast and Teddy was able to feel the unyielding dry land under his feet.

He wondered if his home would be the same.

Perhaps in his absence, his father may even have returned.

Good Lord! There was the baker's shop.

He entered and bought half a dozen rolls.

Then, in his rolling seaman's gait, he made his way to his old house.

Pushing open the door he called out, 'I'm home, Mother!'

A familiar and much-loved voice answered from upstairs, 'Down in a moment, dear.'

And so it was that his mother appeared and looking at her beloved son she remarked, 'Oh good boy, you got the rolls.'

Then noticing her boy's hands – calloused by the sun and sea, crisscrossed with scars, and with his fingernails all black and ingrained with tar, she said:

'Teddy, dear, you really must scrub your hands before going to school!'

The Refugee

....

I asked some of the really old people in the village about the Refugee and his wife. The wife, of course, was also a refugee, but she was known only as "the Refugee's wife".

They just appeared in the village, from who knew where, sometime around 1939, their dark visages suggesting warmer climes, perhaps eastern Europe; he with a black beard and wearing a skipper's hat, she in a long, black dress and headscarf.

He had a few words of English. She – none.

Nobody really knew where they came from – our world seemed to be so much bigger then and, outside the pink areas of the British Empire, there were so many places we knew nothing of – but it was recognised that they must be fleeing from persecution in some foreign land.

Ullapool is like this.

Here we are on what sometimes seems to be the edge of the world and yet our village seems to draw all sorts of unlikely souls.

Some remain, others go on their way.

Ullapool has *always* been like this.

The Refugee must have had some money because not long after their arrival they bought the 'Safeguard' from Alec Ross. She was a small fishing boat which seemed to be permanently propped up alongside the Wee Pier. In fact, one of my earliest memories of Alec Ross was seeing him caulking the gaping seams of the Safeguard – readying her for sale – alongside his brother, George, who was vainly attempting to get her ancient Kelvin engine working.

Well, the sale must have been satisfactorily completed because the Refugee and his wife took up residence in the old boat, making the fish hold into a cabin.

As a child – I was about seven or eight years old – I was never away from the area around the Wee Pier. The shore was my playground and whenever he saw me the Refugee would speak a few words in an English that I could not understand. The lady never spoke but would smile at me, a smile that even a child knew masked sadness.

And so, in a way, I came to know the odd couple.

They busied themselves preparing the Safeguard for sea. Watching as they fitted a mast and sail I wondered what their plans were.

Where did they hope to go?

The construction of the cabin was rough and ready even to my young eyes, but, do you know, that inside it was like a new pin.

How do I know this?

Well, I will tell you.

I too had ambitions to voyage on the great deep seas and had put together a raft from what I had gleaned from the beach – nothing more than a large square board with two long planks beneath.

Keeping close to shore I was able to make short trips, propelling and steering my craft with an old oar. It was more than fine in calm conditions.

On this day, however, a breeze sprang up and the silky water became choppy. The planks started to come out from under the board and, in my frantic efforts to keep the raft together, I allowed my oar to drift away on a wave.

Mercifully, I was still afloat and the raft carried me towards the Wee Pier from where the Refugee and his wife were watching on anxiously.

He started shouting out to me and waving his arms, but then he disappeared below into his boat only to reappear seconds later holding an axe and a plank of wood which he set to work on. I could not think what he was doing and I did not have time to wonder as my vessel was awash and I could not swim.

I didn't need my oar, I needed not to sink.

My voyage came to an abrupt end when I collided, fortunately, with the Wee Pier and found myself clinging to its edge with my head above the water and the raft broken up and swept off in all directions.

The Refugee was too busy at his task to have noticed me but his wife ran down and dragged my shivering body out of the water. Rushing me aboard the boat and into the warmth of the cabin, she dried me off. The towel felt warm and clean and crisp. And I looked around in astonishment at how neat and tidy, and how homely everything was.

The Refugee entered, smiling, and proudly presented me with the new oar he had made.

A bit late, I thought.

And with the ungrateful, but honest, simplicity of a child I said – 'I don't need an oar. I have no ship!'

When the Safeguard was ready to leave, the Refugee asked around the village for a tow to the outer part of Loch Broom, so that he could catch a fair wind to speed them on their way to their destination.

Wherever, that may have been.

Nobody was willing.

The sorry state of the old boat with an engine that would not start, along with the Refugee's obvious lack of seamanship filled the people with dread. To help them leave in such a vessel would be a burden on their conscience. One that they dared not assume.

Eventually, a favourable wind took them away from the Wee Pier and our village, but sadly the Refugee's journey – and that of his wife – ended on the wild, sea-washed rocks of Tanera Beg with the old Safeguard breaking up quickly in the heavy swell. So many months of hard work destroyed in an instant.

But, as they had rescued me, thankfully, so were they rescued, and they were taken to Achilitibuie.

I find myself, all these years later, thinking back to that lady – the Refugee's wife – with her warm towel and sad smile, and her husband too – doggedly working away on that boat in the hope that he could save them from their plight; and I wonder if they ever reached that place they yearned for.

I hope so.

The Loss of the Fairweather V

....

The wreck of the Fairweather V has become a popular
dive site for many divers from around the world.
They come specifically to view what a sea-going
person would think of as the tragic corpse of a
once fine boat. I am told, however, that in her new
incarnation, she is now clothed, bow to stern, in
a beautiful jewelled gown of sea anemones.
The fishermen's loss has become a diver's gain.
Having seen a report about the loss of the above ship,
I would like to tell you of my memory of the event.

This is a true account.

Let me tell you the story of how she went down.
It was February, 1991. I was fast asleep in bed
when the telephone rang – this was not unusual as
often our fast supply boat, the "Bittern" was needed

to service the fleet of Russian and Eastern European klondykers which, at that time, were anchored in Loch Broom.

'Where are you?' the caller demanded.

'I'm in bed!' I replied, still somewhat asleep. Well… it was way past midnight.

'Where is the Bittern?'

'Tied up at the pier. Why?'

'The Fairweather is on the rocks and making water!'

The caller asked that I pick up a pump from the pier and take it to the ship urgently.

'Where is she?' I enquired, hastily slipping from the warm embrace of blankets and wife.

'In the loch!' was the reply.

I rushed down to the pier and was met by Kenny "Skene" who was on duty. He had the pump ready and together we loaded it aboard the Bittern.

Seeing that I was alone he offered – thankfully as it turned out – to sail with me, an offer I gratefully accepted, and so I and this trusty young man set off into the darkness of the night unsure of what we would find at the scene. Given the time of year we were lucky, the weather was at least on our side.

Our information, which was scanty, was that the Fairweather and her partner boat, the Fairwind, were heading back to Peterhead – their home port. As to her actual location at that moment, well we had to guess at it. Our intuition proved correct though, and eventually, we spotted her lights at Carn Dearg rocks in outer Loch Broom.

We found the stricken ship in a truly bad way, her bow hard and high on the rocks, her stern deep with seawater washing over her deck and the stern cabin flooded. At this stage, she had already an enormous amount of water aboard and we realised that the pump we had brought would be totally inadequate.

Kenny and I looked at each other and shook our heads believing, there and then, that nothing could be done to save this ship.

We advised the crew to come aboard the Bittern. This they did.

However, prior to this, the father of the skipper, who was aboard merely to enjoy a peaceful and uneventful trip back to Peterhead in the company of his son, had been placed – in consideration of his age – in the life-raft, which in all the ensuing confusion and panic had drifted away into the darkness.

Fortunately for him, he was picked up by the Fairwind as she hurried to the scene in response to receiving the Fairweather's distress calls.

On arriving she took on board all the Fairweather crew, currently safe on the Bittern, with the exception, unbeknownst to us, of the skipper, who had chosen to return to the wheelhouse of his vessel, in the hope perhaps, that she would float when pulled off the rocks.

Kenny and I were now alone on the Bittern – standing by on the port side and ready to help if necessary.

We watched as the Fairwind nosed up to the stern of the rock-bound ship and a tow line was passed across and made fast.

Gently at first, astern thrust was applied.

The Fairweather did not move. She was stuck fast.

But, the moment the order for "full astern" was given everything happened at once. The stern of the Fairweather juddered and then plunged deep into the ocean shedding all manner of gear onto the surface of the sea.

Only then were we aware that the skipper was still aboard his ship and that he was now needing to be rescued from the starboard side.

The Bittern was at the port side.

We sprang into action, rounding the stern of the Fairwind through all the debris floating on the surface and approached the starboard side of the rapidly sinking ship. The skipper was desperately hanging onto the rail as the bow rose higher and higher. The ship was preparing for her final plunge and very likely, we all thought, she would be taking her master with her.

We nosed into the side of the sinking ship with Kenny hanging over the Bittern's bow, arms outstretched, hoping to get a hold of the skipper before he went down with his ship.

With extraordinary courage and the dexterity of a proper seaman, Kenny leaned dangerously out board and grabbed the man and somehow heaved him in.

Let me say, although this is many years later, a life was saved by that good man.

Danger passed?

No.

As soon as we had the skipper on board we made haste to get clear of the ship's side and went astern on both engines only to have our propellers fouled up in floating ropes from the sinking ship.

As the rope from the Fairweather rapidly spooled down we wondered would we be dragged down too?

Fortune was with us.

There was sufficient length of rope to allow the

Fairweather to settle into her new berth on the seabed and for the Bittern to remain afloat with three very relieved men aboard.

After cutting away all the knots and tangles of rope we were, in our turn, towed home.

On getting home and getting back into my nice warm bed, I still remember my wife, Marjorie, asking me where on earth had I been.

I didn't really know what to say.

Coming from such a chaotic scene and returning to this domestic warmth... well... it felt like I had returned from the moon.

Hearing the horrendous noise of that good vessel slipping to her final resting place is etched, even now, into my mind.

To the great relief of all, she hadn't take anyone of us with her to share her grave – beautiful and peaceful though it may now be.

The Rainbow

....

Four children stand gazing in wide-eyed wonder across the silvery loch. The sun has pierced through a crack in the drizzle-leaden sky, throwing a spear of sunlight onto the Scots pines shrouded in mist on the other side. What in this grey-brown winter landscape could have put such a sparkle in their young eyes? Following their gaze, you would see a rainbow. A beautiful and welcome splash of colour indeed, but just a rainbow I hear you say:

'We *live* in a land of rainbows!'

But this is no ordinary rainbow. Skittering across the sky, turning and flapping – it is more like a fantastical bird with a broken wing.

'She's going to fall!' says the tallest of the boys.

And indeed she does.

Into the trees she goes.

They watch, stricken, as she struggles to escape

her snare, pulling herself into tight, twisting vibrant knots, stretching and snapping her wings. As her colours begin to fade they realise that she is tiring.

Her neck drops into the sea.

'No!' shout the children, 'don't give up!'

Their words float into the cold air, whereupon, a strong breeze blows up and carries them over the water to the rainbow. Hearing them, she rears up into the sky – never had her stripes flashed more brightly – and with one last explosion of energy she snaps her tail away from the needles clutching at her, and sails over to the children waiting on the lochside.

Dipping one end down to their upturned faces, she envelops them in her vivid embrace.

It does seem unbelievable does it not?

And yet here are four children, laughing and hugging her back, and looking through her swirling mists of colour they see... a door?

How very strange.

What should they do?

But let us now meet these children.

Here is Tiger (a name he picked for himself, his parents having wrongly chosen Timothy), and Jennifer, and her two little brothers – Bobby and Roddy.

'Should we open the door?'

Huddling together they discuss the merits – and the dangers.

'What if we end up on another planet,' says Tiger.

That possibility did not appeal to any of them but as they back away they hear a little voice from a loudspeaker set above the door.

'You come in, please?'

It is a welcoming voice, and their curiosity out-weighs their fears and so they open the door.

Rainbow coloured stairs sweep up before them into infinity.

'Phew! This is going to be a long climb,' says Roddy. (Well, he is only a little boy.)

'Don't worry, Roddy,' says Jennifer, 'they are magic stairs. See!'

Sure enough, the stairs carry her up towards the apex of the rainbow.

That's not magic! I hear you say. That's just an escalator, but remember, this was in days long gone by - at least 2BE (2 years Before Escalators!)

At the very top, a little man stands beckoning them on. Even as they approach he doesn't seem to get any bigger, but what he lacks in stature he more than makes up for in appearance. The cocked-hat perched on his head is as tall as his person; his long-tailed coat is of every colour and is stretched tight over his rotund belly; and an impressive waxed moustache – its ends curled up over his pink cheeks – is the very cherry on his round, merry face.

This rainbow of a man is indeed the Captain of this ship.

He looks merrily down on the astonished faces of the children as they rise up to meet him, and as he chuckles the golden epaulettes on his shoulders are sent a-flapping.

'Welcome! Welcome!' he says, ushering them into the wheelhouse, 'Come in, please!'

The soft, hazy walls are lined with cogs and levers, gauges and dials, and pipes and whistles, and in the middle of it all is a mighty ship's wheel and a spinning globe of the world.

Tiger whistles in appreciation.

'Ah, yes!' says the Captain, looking very pleased with himself, 'It is marvellous is it not?'

And he puffs out his chest like a balloon.

The children are, for a moment, awed into silence.

'And I am on a very *momentous* mission. *Very momentous!*' he continued.

'But,' says Tiger, 'how did you manage to get stuck in a tree? And with all these instruments to help you?'

The Captain deflates instantly, 'I do not know how to use all these *fang-dangly* things... and I am ashamed to say it, but I am lost!'

At this, he flings himself on the floor and has a little weep.

'We will help you!' the children chorus, picking him up off the floor, and gently draping him over the Captain's chair.

'What is your mission?'

'What do we have to do?'

Dear readers, you will be happy to know that these bright youngsters soon got the beautiful rainbow ship back into the air where she belonged.

How did they do it?

Well, they did what most adults don't do – they read the instruction manual.

So, now they are rising high above the clouds with two little boys clutching at the enormous wheel, excitedly awaiting orders.

'Where are we heading, Captain?' asks Jennifer.

'The North Pole,' he replies, pointing to the globe spinning slowly above.

Tiger cranks a handle and the globe lowers.

Little flags dot the entire world – Pole to Pole.

'Just what *is* it that you do?' says Tiger, curiously.

'I suppose you could say that I am a delivery man,' replies the Captain sheepishly, and struggling – hopelessly – to contain his modesty he merrily blurts out:

'But a very important one! And I am already behind schedule, so head north, shipmates!'

With these orders duly received Bobby and Roddy point the great ship north-wards, and through the gaps in the clouds they look down on the good people of Ullapool, far below, as they go about their business, entirely ignorant of four children – from their shores – leaving for the North Pole.

As the sun sets on the horizon and the stars come out, the Captain yawns and hoists himself up into his chair. It is warm and snug in the wheelhouse, and the mighty ship is sailing calmly along. The children look out, entranced by the beauty of the blue and green world spinning slowly beneath them.

All the world would seem to be at peace.

A peacefulness broken suddenly by a loud '*HOCHH!*' coming from behind them.

They whip around in alarm, but immediately burst out laughing.

'Shhh!' whispers Jennifer, and points.

There was the Captain, up on his chair with his head under his arm looking altogether like a hen at roost.

Do hens snore?

This one did... and very loudly.

Looking tenderly at their colourful little hen, they turn quietly back to their task.

In the hushed darkness, the little boys too are soon fast asleep, leaving Jennifer and Tiger at the helm. They talk in quiet wonderment of this strange voyage – who would ever believe this story when they could hardly believe it themselves?

Suddenly, the ship judders to a stop. Lights all around the wheelhouse flash amber-red-amber-red, a klaxon belts out an S.O.S. – bah-bah-bah-bip-bip-bip-bah-bah-bah!

The Captain wakes instantly.

'Look!' he says, peering through his telescope into the darkness below, 'There is a ship in distress! Jennifer, stand at the ready, take hold of this lever and, when I pass the order, pull with all your might.'

'Yes, Sir!' she replies.

Tiger, you will then fire the shot!' he says, pointing his finger at a clutter of instruments piled high in the wheelhouse.

Hidden amongst it all they finally make out a gun.

A huge cannon in fact.

With his hands on the wheel and leaning as far out the porthole as his wee body can, the Captain keeps his eye on the stricken ship below whilst steadying the ship

'Get ready!' he says, 'Now, Jennifer... *Pull*!'

Jennifer pulls.

An avalanche of golden coins rattles noisily into the cannon.

'*Fire!*'

Tiger fires.

A rain of gold falls towards the ship.

The children have heard the tales of pots of gold at the end of the rainbow, and indeed they have often dreamt of finding some themselves and becoming rich, but now they are in confusion.

'What use is gold to those poor fisherman?' asks

Jennifer, 'How can gold help them?'

'It is of no use! None at all!' replies the Captain with a twinkle in his eye. 'You cannot eat it, it cannot keep you warm and it certainly cannot stop your boat from sinking.'

He passes her his telescope.

Surveying the scene unfolding below she sees, to her astonishment, the crew waving up at her, smiling and shouting thanks.

'No! A pot of gold is of no use when you are in trouble, but a bilge pump is!' he says, laughing, 'This gold is no ordinary gold, Jennifer. It transforms into whatever is truly needed.'

Hearing these words the children finally understand the importance of their mission, and with that happy realisation on they sail.

High above the frozen Arctic seas, the ship's rainbow lights now shine down through the inky darkness. They see hunters with dogs and sleds, children wrapped up in sealskins, and little houses made of blocks of snow.

'Can we fire?' asks Tiger.

'Of course,' chortles the Captain.

'I wonder what they will magic this into,' said Bobby, craning his neck over to get a better look.

Ah! The gold has become light and fire and fish.

A sea of twinkling candle-light has spread throughout the village. People run out of the gloom and gather together in front of the warm fires now burning, and the children are scampering about, scooping up the rain of golden fish falling onto the ice.

After warm fare-thee-wells on they go once more.

From North to South, in towns and great cities, in little hamlets and villages, in forests and jungle, mountains and green hills, in households both rich and poor, happiness is duly delivered.

At last the time has come for Rainbow's final deliveries in the great deserts of the Sahara. Here, grain stores are replenished with golden wheat, and water wells are filled to overflowing. The little band of travellers watch in delight as children frolic around in the magic of the gentle rain pouring down from the rainbow.

The Captain and his crew are tired but filled with happiness at a job well done.

'Homewards!' shouts the Captain, beaming, and the great ship turns.

As with people, a rainbow cannot survive without water and poor Rainbow is by now dried out and exhausted, the vibrancy of her stripes too have been leached away in the arid lands, she is a like a drawing that has been rubbed away.

Grey and poorly, she has begun to sink.

'We have to refuel!' says the Captain. 'Head for the sea!'

Slowly they make passage for the wild coast of Mauritania. Rainbow limps over the tops of mighty dunes, snagging herself on thorny bushes, and scraping over rocky wastes.

She has become almost invisible.

Almost a ghost.

Will this be their end?

A mist swallows them whole, and they drift along blindly, but then a cold saltiness stings their nostrils.

The sea!

The Atlantic at last!

'Not far to go, Rainbow, you can do it,' shout the children, urging her on.

As the fog clears they skim along the surface of the vast ocean. The damp air soaks into Rainbow like a sponge. Dipping an end into the water she drinks her fill, and as the sun shines down through the sea-mist her colours slowly flicker on one by one – red, orange, yellow, green, blue, indigo and violet.

'Now, Rainbow, let's head home,' said Jennifer, 'your job is done.'

This thought of home fills them with joy, but also anxiety. Each one of them imagines the grief their parents would be feeling at the disappearance of their children.

Oh! They would indeed be sick with worry.

How would they explain their absence?

'Just tell them what happened,' says the Captain, 'they were children once themselves. They will understand that you had to go.'

Let us hope so.

The great ship is now far out into the ocean, but the strong winds which had kindly hustled her southwards are now against her and are blowing ever stronger. Pounded on all sides by this growing tempest, she strains to keep her head into the wind but soon she is spinning like a top. The Captain has tied himself to his wheel and is fighting to keep her under control.

'We need help!' he shouts over the whistling wind, 'Look out below and see if you can see a ship.'

Oh, dear! They are in trouble now.

What on earth is Jennifer doing?

Clutching and stumbling past gauges and levers, past the whirling wind speed anemometer, she has found what she is looking for. A switch marked – just as she had read on page 53 of the instruction manual – "Whale Speaker".

'Hello!' she shouts into the mouthpiece, 'Hello, Whale!'

It crackles loudly, but there is no reply.

Their hearts sink.

Would ever see their families again?

'We have to shout together – as loudly as we can!' says Jennifer.

'Hello, Whale!!!' they bellow.

Finally, through the crackling wire, and sounding as though it was coming from a million fathoms away – they hear a deep, but broken up, call.

A whale?

Is it possible?

'Please help us!' pleads Jennifer, 'We are in terrible trouble and cannot make headway. Can you tow us home to Ullapool?'

'I *am* going that way,' comes the voice from afar, 'Throw down a rope!'

And peering through the darkness of the tempest and the slanting rain they see their good samaritan – a whale indeed.

A *huge* whale - but even a whale is but a tiny speck in the vastness of an ocean.

I tell you, folks, it was no easy job and, after several tries at throwing down the rope, they soon realised that someone would have to be lowered down to make it fast around the whale.

Little Roddy, the smallest of them all speaks out:

'I'll do it. I'm not afraid! Not *really*.'

'He will be fine,' says the Captain, surveying their worried faces, 'Let him go.'

Carefully, they lower the lad down through the wild night onto the whale's back. Slipping and sliding he runs the length of the whale rope in hand, and standing in the wind he fashions a noose and flings it out over the enormous head.

The whale looks on with concern as the boy slowly clambers back up the slippery rope to the ship.

Struggling hard, he is now within reach of Rainbow's port-side door.

The wind is immense and he's ripping and flapping about like a flag. The boy stretches out his small hand, and as he strives to grab the outstretched hands before him, he slips and falls.

'Roddy!' they scream.

The Captain sobs.

He has never before had a crew, and now he has lost one of them.

But the whale has not for one moment taken his eye of the brave lad, and watching him tumble down through the stormy night, he waits for the boy to fall upon him. In the fraction of the second before he hits the whale, the whale exhales through his blowhole with all his mighty might:

PHWOAR!

Roddy soars up into the air like a rocket, atop a powerful column of vapour. The children reach out with all hands once more and haul the drenched and shivering boy back into the safety of the Rainbow.

The Captain cries even more.

The great Leviathan below now takes up the slack, and using all his strength he slowly pulls Rainbow northwards, through the tempest and the high seas until, at last, they pull into the silvery tranquil waters of Loch Broom.

Through the Whale Speaker they hear the distant song of their friend as he calls out goodbye and slips free of the rope.

'Thank you, Whale!' they shout in reply.

Now comes the time for the Captain and the children to part ways and say their own farewells.

There are many tears, of course, as they part – the Captain's eyes like two spouting spigots, and Rainbow?... well she rained.

The children, though sad to go, are thankful to be home, and proud too of having played a part in such an adventure.

And so, one by one, they slide down Rainbow and plop into their soft warm beds, immediately falling into a deep sleep.

I see that they are dreaming about rainbows and storms, deserts and ice, and whales, and a funny little Captain, and I see, too, that they each one is clutching something in their hand.

What might that be?

Ah!

A little golden coin.

A House for the Manager

....

The estate was quite a large property and had been owned by the same family for generations; it was now run fairly and reliably by the last surviving member of that family, Mr. Rupert Hudson.

Mr. Hudson had recently been to see his doctor in the nearby town, and as a result of the doctor's advice was feeling a bit upset.

The doctor, also his friend, had put it bluntly, 'You are getting too old for managing that high estate, Rupert. You must take it easy, or I'll soon be signing your final certificate! Get a younger man to look after the place.'

There was no doubt in Hudson's mind that he had been feeling the weight of his years recently.

Perhaps that old fool, Doctor Mathieson, might for once be right, and so, in his mind, he decided to look out for a suitable person to manage the estate.

But first, he thought, he would have to build a house for this new person.

The estate had quite a large labour force, as was normal in those bygone days before modern mechanisation took over and in charge of the workers was the general foreman, John Forbes, a dependable man of forty years of age who was able to turn his hand to anything.

John Forbes was summoned to the big house to discuss events. Mr. Hudson informed his foreman that he was considering taking on a manager to help him run the estate and that he would require a new house to be built, suitable for this new and most important employee.

John Forbes agreed that Mr. Hudson was correct in his aims, then suggested that he would be pleased to supervise the building of a suitable house.

With the plans duly drawn up, Mr. Hudson and his Foreman carefully went over them and were of one and the same opinion – it was most acceptable.

'Now, John,' said Mr. Hudson, 'I'm going to leave the building of it entirely in your hands. I know that you will see it sensibly built and that it will be a comfortable and welcoming residence for the new man, whoever he may be.'

As we know, building a house is not done overnight – but John Forbes did his best to progress the work quickly and efficiently, he was careful to ensure that a lovely site was located on the estate and that the foundations were dug out accurately and laid level with corners of 90 degrees exactly.

Much of the material for the building was available from the estate itself. The stone was cut in the quarry, the timber was felled from the large forest around and was worked on in the estate sawmill.

Under John's critical eye things went well and in good time the house began to take shape with some very handsome, random stonework and a splendid slated roof. It was evident to all who saw it that this would be a lovely house for a very lucky man.

Although he was the boss, Mr. Hudson was true to his word and did not once interfere with the work, accepting John Forbes' accounts for all money spent without a single comment.

And then the house was finished – all neat and tidy, outside and in. The foreman and his men were content that a good sound job had been done and were more than hopeful that the boss would agree when he came to inspect the new build.

John Forbes was a little concerned though, as he marched up to the big house with the key, that the boss had never once come to have a look at the work whilst it was in progress. He hoped that he had built a house that both Mr. Hudson and the new manager would find suitable and welcoming.

'Finished it, then John?' exclaimed Mr. Hudson, 'Let's go down and have a look shall we.'

This they did, with John pointing out everything of interest to a seemingly disinterested Mr. Hudson.

'Well, Mr. Hudson,' said his general foreman, slightly irritated by the lack of comment on all the good work done, 'Are you satisfied?'

Mr. Hudson turned to John Forbes, saying, 'I cannot fault this splendid house you have built, and no doubt any manager would be pleased to live here. Well done to you and your men.'

With certain relief, John was pleased, proud of his builders and of himself. He had done his best and it should be said that his best was extremely well done.

'By the way Mr. Hudson, when do you expect the new man to arrive?' asked John.

For the first time, Mr. Hudson smiled.

'Ah! But he's already here, John. And I can now shake hands with the new manager in this lovely house which you have worked so hard on!'

His smile grew from ear to ear.

'Welcome home, John, this is your house now, where I hope you and your family will be happy and remain, as long as you wish, to look after the estate.'

Laughing, they grasped each other's hands and shook warmly and, on throwing open the front door to the beautiful outlook, they were both aware of a spirit of happiness and good luck entering and taking up residence in this new home.

The Black Pearl

. . . .

At one time travelling folk journeyed from lochan to river looking for pearls. They waded and dived in the fast-flowing clear waters in search of freshwater mussels which would, on occasion, contain treasure.

As ever, over-fishing of the freshwater mussels reduced their numbers to such an extent that this type of activity was banned and in fact is still no longer permitted. But, memories live on. Memories of what seem to be the eternal golden years of youth; of camping by rivers and streams; of the sun shining all summer long; of living off the land with the odd hare or rabbit roasting in the pot, or a trout or two sizzling in the frying pan; of the family lounging on the green sward alongside the stream without a care in the world; and, of course, of the mussels and the hope, that on the opening of that indigo blue teardrop of a shell a perfect pearl would be found.

Good old days, long gone but well-remembered.

In the wee council cottage, occupied by Rory and Alana, these thoughts of bygone days filled them with pleasure. They were both from a long line of travelling families – Rory of the MacAlistair clan and Alana of the O'Donnells.

They had been together, with not one day apart, since both were sixteen years old; and wending their way through the highlands in the company of other such families, they would make camp in secret spots known only to them, places now fondly remembered in tales of long ago.

Now cooped up in this little house for what might be the rest of their days these dreams, of a time when only the seasons governed their youthful lives, became a haven, a place to be young once more.

It was spring now and, despite their old age and the sluggish blood flowing in their veins, these two old folk felt an awakening – an inborn urge to take to the road once more.

They looked at one another and Alana, with her flashing fresh eyes, suggested to her beloved husband, 'Come on, Rory, we're not dead yet. Get the old car out and we'll be off from here.'

Rory needed no further urging, so the old couple set too with a will, quickly packing up the few things that their spartan lives had need of. The old bell tent was fine and, of course, he could not forget his fishing gear – the rod and landing net – and just for the fun of it, he thought, he would take the glass-bottomed box which in times gone by he had used to locate the mussels on the river bed; and, well, in that case, he should take his old shelling knife too.

You never know, do you?

The rusty old car was soon packed up ready to go and, with the way north beckoning them on, they took off. With the passing of each day on the road, Alana and Rory's spirits soared. They stopped at old places, rekindling their memories and amiably chatting together about the pearls they had fished for.

'Remember, Rory, the grand wee site north of Ullapool where the road branches off to Rhue?'

'Indeed I do, Alana,' he replied, 'Well, lass, we'll head for that place, shall we?

She nodded happily.

'Mind you, it was not much good for pearls, was it? – Ah, but then that's all finished now,' he remarked a little ruefully.

His spirits, buoyant as they were, instantly perked back up and answering his own misgivings he said, 'But you never know what's in store! And there used to be good fishing for trout there too – in that wee pool down there by the sea.'

With these happy thoughts, they journeyed on.

It was evening when they arrived at their longed-for destination and they were exultant in the fact that it had not much changed. Well, the bridge had been replaced, but their site was still the same so, with glee, they hastily unloaded the car and humped their gear to the very place they had occupied all those years ago – down by the burn – and set up camp.

In no time at all the canvas bell tent was erected, a little fire of twigs was lit and the old iron kettle, with its belly full of clear water from the burn, was steaming away ready for a brew. After their long day on the road, the old travellers were tired and after their supper were both eager to turn in for the night under the shelter of their tent.

In that joyful peace, they lay back sleepily.

'Remember to switch off the light, Rory!' joked Alana, warmly.

'Och aye, Alana, that I will!' Rory sleepily replied, and with their hands entwined they drifted off to dreamland, cushioned by the soft wad of thick green moss beneath them.

There was not much darkness in the long summer nights, but despite this, the old couple slept well, awakening early to birdsong. Looking out through the triangular flap of the tent they could see the dawning of another perfect day.

They rose together.

Alana raked in the embers of last night's fire and fanning the still hot ashes carefully while adding dry grass and twigs, she revived the flames.

The blackened kettle was soon boiling for tea and, of course, there was their breakfast brose to look forward to – a simple bowl of oatmeal and hot water with perhaps a spoonful of syrup added. As ever, this would sustain them for the whole day if need be, but hopefully, Rory would catch a trout or two before evening. Alana thought that very likely; he had never disappointed her before after all.

Rory could see from the burn that there had not been much rain recently, but he recollected that there was a deep pool further down, nearer the sea.

Worth a look, he thought.

He donned his waterproof trousers and opening the car boot took out the glass-bottomed box and the landing net in the hope that there might be a trout to be flipped out. And what about the knife? With its curved blade and the wood handle that had worn down over many a year, it fit so perfectly his grasp.

Well?

Might he need it?

There may be a few freshwater mussels.

So, however unlikely, he stowed his shelling knife in his pocket. He felt grand and with a spring in his step, he set off for the sea pool.

Arriving at the pool he readied himself, his eyes slowly scanning the water, already noting the oscillating fin marks radiating out on the calm surface as the tide-trapped fish swam lazily around below awaiting the returning tide to rise up and release them.

He stepped cautiously into the dark water and lowering his box onto the surface he bent over and looked through the glass to see the bed of the pool, where to his joy he spotted several good-sized sea trout darting away. From his years of experience Rory had evolved a technique with which he was able to corner, first one fish, and then another and with a quick flip of the landing net, they would find themselves high and dry on the bank.

Supper is assured, thought the fisherman with much satisfaction.

As to freshwater mussels, Rory was not too hopeful. This pool was too near to the sea, but there was no harm in having a look. Slowly moving the box over the surface he searched methodically, but without success. What was this black object that he kept passing over though? Just a stone probably, but it was unusual. He prodded it with the handle of the landing net. It did not move. He raked the gravel from around it. Still, he could not move it.

'Strange,' muttered Rory, now determined to get

this pebble to the surface. Bending down deeply into the water he managed to grasp the stone and, although it proved difficult, he finally managed to heave it up from the bed of the pool.

The stone, which was about the size of a hen's egg, was astonishingly heavy and in the sharp, clear air of the day Rory was struck by the intensity of its blackness – so dark was it that, even though the sun shone upon its surface, it did not reflect any light back. In a lifetime exploring the shallow fresh waters Rory had never seen the like.

What would Alana think of it, he wondered, and with that thought, he picked up the trout and his gear, and with the black pebble weighing heavily in his pocket, he hurried back.

Alana viewed her husband's return with pleasure, especially his offering of the two splendid fish which she would prepare for their supper, but when he showed her the 'pearl' he saw her recoil in horror.

'I'm not keen on that... *thing*, Rory,' she said in concern, feeling a heaviness take root in her heart.

'And why are you calling it a pearl? It's not and never has been a pearl... *a pearl indeed!*'

From deep within her there flowed a sense of foreboding, she was conscious of a power, of an energy being emitted; holding it in her hand, she felt a burning heat rise from within.

She threw it to the ground, and cried out to Rory:

'It's cursed - you must return it from wherever it came!'

Rory was upset at Alana's reaction to his mysterious find. He too sensed its power, a power he felt even more on holding it close; he felt his old body absorb the fiery heat and it made him feel good. He felt the years fall away.

He felt young once more.

There was no way was he going to take it back.

Much to Alana's annoyance, Rory made a small pouch to contain it and this he wore on a stout cord around his neck, well out of Alana's reach.

The days passed in good weather and while the old travellers enjoyed being there and living off the land there was a sea-change in their normally close relationship. Alana looked more and more strained and worried, and somehow older than her many years, while inversely, Rory became the very epitome of youth. He charged about, running down the path to the sea and swimming in the cold salt water.

So many years had passed since he had felt thus.

Alana, in her dread, knew this change was due to the pearl. All she wanted was the Rory she had known and loved for more than half a century, not this strange, newly young – but yet old – man.

The pearl hung tantalisingly close, but was safely out of her reach. She refused to think of that abhorrent thing as a pearl – a pearl is beautiful, a lustrous, light, silken drop, the very opposite of this dead, black stone.

It's evil, she thought and, unable to stop muttering these words over and over, she wondered how she could gain possession of it.

On their last day there, Rory, bursting with life, suggested that before leaving they should visit the trout pool once more. Secretly, he hoped against hope that there may be another black pearl in the pool bed. Would it not be wonderful if he found one for his beloved Alana?

Off they went, Rory rushing down in his eagerness

to get into the water with Alana following stiffly and slowly, yet watchfully, behind. She sat nervously on the bank as her man kitted up for his last survey of the pool.

She watched as Rory bent over the surface of the pool to peer through the glass box. She gazed raptly at the hated stone hanging about his neck. As he moved the black pearl swayed like a pendulum. Not taking her eyes off it for even a second, she watched in horror as all of a sudden it swung out. Wheeling and spinning around and around Rory's throat, it was strangling him, and hauling him ever deeper into the water.

The pearl had a life of its own, and that life was Rory's. In seconds all that could be seen of Rory were his legs thrashing at the surface of the dark and turbulent pool.

Screaming, Alana rushed into the water. She attempted to raise his head above the surface, but whatever force was being used to drown Rory it was too much for Alana, even had she been young once more.

She knew that she had to cut that encircling cord. Remembering Rory's old shelling knife she desperately reached into his pocket and drawing it out she slashed blindly at the necklace.

Blood spurted from the wound she gave him, swirling and staining the water deep red, but finally the cord was cut and the pearl dropped away.

Rory was released from its deadly hold.

Alana, using every ounce of strength that was left in her frail, old body, dragged her still-living man from the pool.

Now freed from the pearl, and with his neck

bandaged up with a piece of cloth his wife had torn from her skirt, Rory a moment of clarity – his fragmented thoughts coalesced into a single vision, and looking into his wife's face he saw her as he had seen her for the first time.

How beautiful she had been.

And he saw her as she was now. Her beauty was there still. Young, old – she was one and the same.

How much he owed this, his lifetime, partner – his beloved Alana.

He thought of all the years that they had shared together – how happy he had been with her and now that their lives had returned to normal, well… he was even happier, old though they both still were.

Shaken and exhausted by the near-tragic events of the day they did not attempt to leave; instead they sat looking out over the sea, watching as the sun sank slowly over the horizon, and with the fire burning hot and bright they talked long into the dusky, summer twilight – remembering the far-off, golden days of their youth, when together they had searched for pearls, here in this land.

Together then and together once more.

Baldy and Rover

....

Picture the scene: two young children playing at the wee pier in the drowsy peace of a summer morning. These two little people, Abie and Nabbie, played at the water's edge, and watched as the tide crept in and floated the few boats, which now bobbed at their moorings awaiting their owner's arrival. It was a grand day, a perfect day to catch a bucket-full of haddies in the pools and pollans of Loch Broom.

The children caught sight of an elderly man as he strode down Mill Street, past the graveyard.

I say elderly, but thinking back, to their young eyes anyone over thirty was thought of as such, so it is hard to know now just how old this old man may have been. Anyway, the little girl recognised the figure at once, dressed as he was in his fisherman's garb – long, sloppy, rubber-boots, an oilskin jacket and a tweed cap to protect what she knew to be his completely hairless head from whatever weather prevailed. He carried under his arm a basket full of hooks and line.

They cast their eyes around somewhat anxiously. Where was the fisherman's mate?

The man smiled down at their upturned, quizzical faces, and greeted them in the familiar and friendly way one did in those days when everyone knew everyone else, and could readily identify the tangled strands that wove the families of the village together.

Baldy, as he was affectionately known – pulled his boat in and carefully placed his basket in the bow. The children cast their eyes over the street once more before calling out in unison:

'Where is Rover?'

Surely Baldy would not be going out without him.

It was unthinkable. Everyone knew that Baldy needed his crewman.

Baldy chuckled at the children's concern.

'Don't worry, he'll be down soon! He's probably met one of his friends. You know how he is.'

That was true, the children agreed, he was known for his love of wandering. Maybe that was how he had gained his name, they mused.

And sure enough, as if by magic, Rover sauntered into view. Young and agile, he was full of the joys of spring, leaping on and off the pier with ease. His bright, shining brown eyes took in everything around him and in his black and white coat, which was unusual attire for a fisherman, he was a picture of elegance.

Enchanted, the children set about him in excitement, jumping around and chasing after him, although he was too fast for them to ever catch.

But with some impatience, Baldy called out, 'Come on, boy! The fish are waiting!'

Rover had to say his goodbyes.

In his headlong dash for the boat he knocked the wee boy down, but this was quickly followed by screams of laughter as Rover then thrust his long, wet, nose into the gleeful little face and gave him a big, slobbery lick.

Ah, dear readers, you may already have guessed that this particular fisherman was of the four-legged variety. Indeed, he was a very handsome springer spaniel, and an intelligent one too, because on hearing Baldy's words he was now keenly aware that he was a little late for duty, and so, after the elderly fisherman had clambered stiffly over the stem Rover seemed to take to the air, and flying over the gunwale he eagerly assumed his usual position. Putting aside his hitherto playfulness he placed his paw diligently on the tiller, and with true professionalism he calmly got ready to set out to sea.

Baldy hoisted the sail. The wind filled it nicely, pushing them gently towards their favourite fishing spot.

Spellbound, the two little figures watched from the pier as Rover – with his big, soft, spaniel paw – lightly and feelingly steered the boat away, sniffing the wind and earnestly watching his captain as he baited the lines. Occasionally Baldy would indicate – with a gentle word, or a mere wave of his hand – that a minor adjustment to the course was needed. Rover immediately adjusted the tiller – he never had to be asked twice. The two worked as one.

In complete harmony.

On this lovely morning Rover, keenly conscious

that he was being watched, albeit by a couple of urchins, looked back over his shoulder and, of all things... smiled.

The children laughed and jumped up and down with delight.

'Oh, what a magical dog you are!' cried Abie.

And they watched the little boat – and her 'odd couple' of a crew – sail swiftly away.

The Forsyth Saga

....

When we were children much of the village milk came from Leckmelm Farm and was delivered to every doorstep by Findlay Forsyth, driving his horse and trap. The milk was contained in a large drum mounted within the trap and was dispensed through a brass tap into whatever container the customer kept for the purpose – usually a tin pail, the upturned lid of which held the money to pay for the milk.

The system worked well, with Findlay regular as clockwork in all weathers and him never wearing a coat or anything, but always cheerful.

Of course, the horse knew the milk round just as well as Findlay himself, maybe even better, and would stop automatically at the customers' doors without the slightest command.

Coming home from school in the afternoon one fine day, the boys were surprised to see the milkman's horse, with the trap still coupled to it, peacefully grazing away on that little patch of grass that used to exist outside the Royal Bank of Scotland's garden wall on Argyle Street.

They wondered if Findlay was in the bank, depositing the takings.

'No,' said one, 'it's closed now. Perhaps Findlay has forgotten the horse and has got a lift back to Leckmelm?'

Unlikely, they thought.

'Ask the horse!' said one young joker.

They all knew the horse and the pleasant good-natured beast knew the boys. The horse also knew that he was fed up waiting for Findlay and was anxious to get back to Leckmelm where decent fare would be available, rather than this downtrodden muddy grass. He knew too, exactly where Findlay was but chose not to reveal it.

Chewing away at the tough grass he remembered that this had happened before.

While Findlay was probably okay, he thought, perhaps he needed to be reminded that horses have rights too.

To their credit the boys felt that they should do something helpful, thinking that some harm might come to the animal, free as he was. Perhaps they could somehow shift the horse and trap to a safer location – a field or something.

The Shore Street boys knew nothing about manoeuvring a horse, especially one with a trailer hanging onto it. Being shore boys they thought in nautical terms, so they mused amongst themselves about what one had to do to make the horse go ahead or – even trickier – go astern.

What do you do when there is no wheel or tiller to guide your direction, they wondered.

Fortunately, among these boys, there was one from Market Street who had left his territory for an hour or two. He looked at these ignorant Shore Street boys with contempt and thought about how they lived right up against that huge puddle which would come in and go out, day in day out, threatening to inundate the houses and drown the people... and them so snooty too.

He was glad that he lived in calmer conditions and he certainly knew a lot more about animals and milk floats than these Shore Street urchins.

He could show them a thing or two.

'Look!' he said to the small crowd of boys, 'First I'll get a grip of the horse's head and walk him around gently until he's pointing in the right direction.'

This he did, making it look so easy.

'But how do you get it started to go ahead?' asked one of the Shore Street kids.

The Market Street boy pointed out the two ropes leading to the animal's head saying, 'You just flap them and the horse will move forward.'

'Cor!' the Shore Street boys chorused, 'Nothing difficult about that.'

Instantly one of them grabbed at the ropes and, vigorously flapping them, he indicated to the animal, in no uncertain terms, that it was time to be on his way, Findlay or no Findlay.

Time to teach this young upstart a lesson thought the horse, annoyed at this rough treatment and leaping forward and gaining speed as he went, he took off in a headlong, clattering dash along Argyle Street.

Within the quiet, dark confines of the Argyll bar, the gathered throng heard the clattering hooves as the milk horse thundered towards them with the empty milk drum clanking around noisily in the bumping trap. This raucous cacophony broke into Findlay's, hitherto peaceful, perusal of the pint standing in front of him, moreover, the excited shouts of the schoolboys gave further note that something most unusual was occurring outside.

Findlay's head shot up.

He recognised that these sounds spelt trouble.

Making haste to down his glass to the dregs, he shouldered his way clumsily to the exit only to see the milk float rattling speedily by.

'Stop!' he shouted.

And – for a just one moment – it seemed that his command had been heeded and that the trap was, in fact, slowing down.

Indeed, the horse did pause on hearing the gruff, familiar voice of his master, but only to protest in a way that his master might understand...

He loudly broke wind.

A rather rude and noisy retort to your master maybe, but needs must.

'It's that rubbish grass,' thought the horse galloping on for Leckmelm and his nice bale of sweet hay.

Findlay shook his head and re-entered the bar.

'Just one for the road,' he muttered meekly to a grinning barman.

Gold at Braes?

....

There have always been rumours that gold existed in the Braes area of Ullapool and perhaps it does, albeit in small quantities. The most likely place to go looking, and perhaps do a bit of panning, would be alongside the little burn chuckling its way seawards, past Allan's house and onwards to the old mill standing at the edge of the loch.

Think, dear reader, of those delicate glittering flecks, and maybe a rare chunky nugget worked out of the silty soil by heavy rain, sweeping and clinking their way over rocky edges and sinking to the bottom of the immense ocean seabed – lost for evermore.

Gold there might be, and gold there surely is, so let me tell you what I know of it.

High up on the skyline above Dunky Jeck's house you may have noticed the ruins of an old crofthouse. Long ago this place was occupied by a poor family –

the MacBahns – and their young son, Daniel.

From this otherworldly place, you can look at the world unfurling far beyond. Around the ruin, one can still see where the land was cultivated, flat and grassy as it is. There was just enough there for the people to eke out a living and the couple looked forward to the time that their boy would be old enough to help with the hard work of the croft.

Sadly, the boy, Daniel, had no interest in being a crofter, only wishing to leave this lonely place.

Standing on the rocky summit gazing out over the beautiful loch spreading onwards before him, around and beyond the faraway islands, he thought:

Tis the pathway to everywhere.

That is my path.

When the Dutch lugger left the pier at Ullapool, heavily laden with salted Loch Broom herring, the young Daniel MacBahn was aboard, signed on as a cabin boy, leaving his distraught parents alone on the windswept heights of Braes. They watched in their misery as the lugger made sail bearing their boy, and their hopes, away.

The woman cried, 'He'll never come back, Calum.'

Calum's head slumped in grief.

They were wrong.

Eventually, Daniel did return, but sadly, long after they had both departed this world.

Anyway, so began a seafaring life.

The young Daniel evolved from a skinny runt of a cabin boy into a rock-hard sailor man and, as such, he served on many ships, ploughing an endless looping furrow through the world's oceans to the many exotic foreign ports of the empire and beyond.

Never attaining command, but being a splendid

seaman, he often held the rank of Bosun in charge of the deck crew – these men were, in fact, the engine of any ship dependent on wind and sails for its momentum through the water and Daniel became a hard man indeed, his orders were obeyed with alacrity, or else fists were administered.

Many years passed and now we join Daniel in Liverpool, having been just paid off from his latest ship. Here he is – pockets full of cash and making haste for the nearest hostelry, where a good time was guaranteed, even for a middle-aged seaman – as he now was.

Did he ever consider journeying north to his home? He did, but first, some merriment was to be had. Before long his money was in other people's pockets and Daniel's were empty.

He couldn't go home now.

The story of my life, he thought soberly, and guiltily, as he paced along the quay looking for a new berth.

One more voyage and I'll head north for sure, he promised himself – and his parents.

They could not hear him, both being long gone.

He shouted down to a loaded ship that was ready to sail and easily securing the job of Bosun.

'Come aboard,' growled the Mate seeing a good seaman before him.

The ship was bound for California loaded with supplies for the goldmines. It would be a long voyage round the Horn and up the west coast of the Americas – a long and dangerous voyage, but it would be a good payer – if he survived.

'More days, more dollars,' Daniel sighed to himself, gratefully dropping his gear aboard.

In the hundred days the ship took to reach her destination, the crew were fortunate with the weather. Even the rounding of the dreaded Horn was accomplished without damage to the ship, the rigging, or the men.

After such a long time at sea, the crew were anxious to get ashore in San Francisco. The captain, though, had different ideas and made it clear that their wages would not be paid until their return to Liverpool. He was worried that many would desert ship and go to the goldmines.

This was in fact what our Daniel was planning, and he did indeed leave the ship – along with many others – even though he had not a penny. All the stories that he had heard of the riches waiting to be found were just too great a temptation to resist.

Secretly, at dead of night, while the ship lay at anchor awaiting discharge of cargo, he slipped into the sea and swam strongly to the shore, and before long was heading for the mines.

In the months following, the hardened seaman became a hardened miner, and working doggedly at his claim – and with a good amount of luck – he struck a vein of the precious metal. He mined all the gold he could and jealously secreted it away. Now, if he could avoid the many thieves about and get a berth on a returning ship, he would return home a rich man indeed.

Craftily, he let it be known that he had found nothing, that he was indeed destitute, and that he would have to sell off all his tools. These tools were eagerly purchased by yet another wave of newly arrived prospectors, and once rid of them he set off down-river to the port, from where he might obtain a berth on a British vessel returning home.

At the port, Daniel used some of the money he had made from the sale of the mining gear to purchase clothing suitable for a seaman, including a thick, warm, woollen jacket.

Looking over the many ships marooned in the harbour for lack of men to sail them, he knew that he would get a berth easily and, as expected, two days later he was back at sea sailing south.

This time the tip of South America was in a foul mood and they were pounded by ferocious storms and heavy seas. Even as a lifelong seaman Daniel wondered if he would ever see his homeland again. In the snow-swept, gale-lashed, roaring forties he had at least his warm coat to wrap around him.

Cape Horn bettered and with a southerly wind astern, the ship now made speed north into warmer weather. The crew looked askance at their Bosun as he drove them on.

How could he bear to wear that salt and wind ravaged coat in this now much balmier clime, they asked themselves.

He even slept in the bloody thing, they said, but this was whispered well out of earshot – and while standing well to windward – of that stinking bear of a man.

'Its woolly weight keeps me stable on deck,' he would say when asked if he was not too warm in it.

In fact, prior to boarding his new ship, he had done some neat tailor work on the jacket and it was now lined with his hard found gold.

This was the weight that kept him anchored to the deck, and anchored to his thoughts of home.

It was a weight he was happy to shoulder.

Through the heat of the tropics, the ship drove on and at last arrived at the mouth of the Mersey, to the joy of everyone on board, especially Daniel, chaffed and crippled as he was by the constant sweat-dampened, foetid weight of his coat.

He determined though, that he would keep it on until he was safe in his homeland.

Once alongside at Liverpool, as is usual, the ship paid off and now we have Daniel with actual money in his pockets.

Did he go to his favourite hostelry for an almighty good time, drinking and gambling?

No.

He was a changed man, and with the state that he was in – with that stinking, old, raggedy jacket hanging off him – well...even there, in that lowly place, he would not be well received.

Anyone who saw him could only but describe him as a tramp, and it was as such that he chose to be seen, at least until he arrived at his still distant but ever closer homeland. With every mile that passed, more and more bowed down was he – his coat now forming a hide-like skin around his tired-out body.

Wearily he trudged on.

Naturally, the Braes residents noticed the tramp dragging himself through the sparsely-populated area. They were compassionate people and would gladly have shared food with this poor, worn-out, shadow of a man.

Curiously the tramp seemed to know where he was going and he paid no heed to those he passed amongst; instead, he slogged on towards the old MacBhan's crofthouse which now lay in ruins.

Daniel had now reached journey's end and with

emotion his fingers traced the ancient stonework of the house in which he had been born, and he remembered his happy childhood and his loving, if overly protective, parents.

The house was deserted.

His heart was as heavy as lead. He didn't need anyone to tell him that they had passed on. They would never have left their croft and their land, and each day they would have hoped for his return.

Now all was gone.

This hard, but weary, man was consumed with guilt at what he now saw had been a wasted and selfish life – and with nothing to show for it but that accursed gold.

What use was it now to those loved ones long departed – much less to himself?

He no longer saw himself as a rich man.

He had been a Braes man, and this he hoped to be once more.

He would live among his own people at last.

Daniel walked the short distance to the cliff edge from whence he had viewed his path out of here so many lifetimes ago, and for the first time in months, he unfastened the woollen jacket, letting the heavy burden slip from his shoulders.

He felt his body lighten, so much so that he felt that he would float up to the skies.

Taking a huge breath, he filled his lungs with the sweet Braes air and shouted, 'I'm home!'

The curse of the gold lifted and Daniel set about re-establishing his old home with the kindly help of his neighbours, and in time he brought the place to life once again.

His parents, had they still been alive, would have

been proud.

So that no others could be infected by the poison of that cursed gold, he stashed his hard-won treasure – still contained within that awful, malevolent jacket – in a nearby cave and covered it with great heavy stones and walked away.

It would never arise again.

ULLAPOOL 1939

As children, my brother Johnny and I loved to roam the hills and on this one particular day, we pondered where we should go to explore. We knew where Charlie's Cave was as we had often heard it talked about, and we wondered if indeed Prince Charlie had hidden there in 1746, after his routing at the battle of Culloden.

We decided to go and have a look at the place, we might even find some evidence of the Prince's presence. A brass button or a belt buckle.

We armed ourselves with a torch and our Father's Sunday walking stick – the one with the dog's head carved into the handle. It might come in handy, we thought, and so provided off we set.

Going up by Fairy Dell we were not long in reaching the cave and we crawled into its dark outer cavern. Using the torch we thoroughly examined the chamber – not a sign of the Prince's occupation; however, at one end we noticed a pile of stones and remembered hearing that these had been placed so that animals – or even small boys – might not fall into the deep interior.

What to do, we thought.

To do a proper survey we would have to shift the stones. This we did. It was heavy work, but Father's

Sunday walking stick proved handy as a lever. Soon the dark hole was revealed, but at that very moment the torch failed and all we could see of the inner cave was a rocky ledge, beyond that was complete blackness.

We chucked a few stones in and listened to them bounce off the rocky wall before eventually hearing them splash somewhere far below.

Using the stick once more we probed the darkness and Johnny announced that on the ledge he could feel something soft.

Perhaps a sheepskin, we thought, maybe Prince Charlie used a sheepskin to keep warm.

We took turns prodding it some more.

It smelled bad.

But our curiosity knew no bounds, and so turning the stick around Johnny tried to pull whatever it was out with the dog's-head handle, but it was heavy and it wouldn't move.

And the more we tried to shift it the more it stank.

Holding our noses we kept on trying but to no avail. Whatever that rank thing was we were not going to be able to pull it out of the cave and worse, it was now polluting the chamber with that rank, awful, dead smell.

Retching and revolted though we both were, but wanting to keep the purity of the cave intact, we decided that with a hard enough push we could dislodge the foul thing and it would fall into the water far below in the darkness.

The sharp end of the stick was useless, so the dog's head went in. Together we pushed and pushed and our efforts were at last rewarded when the abhorrent article finally slithered off, followed some seconds later by a satisfying splash echoing back from the very deepest of depths.

The air was once more sweet and pure.

We rejoiced as we clambered out.

But in our jubilant celebration of a deed well done, we almost forgot Father's precious stick.

I ducked back in and handed it out to my brother.

Aww... it smelled awful.

We would have to clean it up.

Taking it to a stream we washed it carefully, wondering at the hundreds and thousands of little, golden flecks embedded in the nooks and crannies of the dog's head and eyes.

After giving it a good scrub with heather, we breathed a sigh of relief – the glittering flecks were finally gone.

Father would not notice, we thought happily.

He is fussy about his dog's-head walking stick.

Chuckles in Church

....

In my youth, most people in Ullapool attended church, at one or other of the various places of worship. Our family was no exception, dutifully visiting the Church of Scotland on a reasonably regular basis.

At this church, the congregation enjoyed the music of the organ and the singing of the choir, but on one Sunday there was a problem.

Let me explain.

In these wartime days the village was very quiet with many of the younger people away on active service, but because of occasional heavy landings of herring, the pier offered part-time employment to any available men to handle the fish.

This being wartime, food was rationed.

Even herring was valued.

One of these men was Willie Bruce, who was an

older incomer from the east coast of Scotland – he was a man eager to help with jobs around the pier, and eager also to take part in village life which included churchgoing. Here he blessed the congregation with his presence and, in the community singing within that church, he blessed them with his voice.

He wondered, hopefully, if perhaps the choirmaster might recognise the quality of his singing and invite him to join the choir, but so far this had not happened.

And *would* not, thought the choirmaster.

As is usual in Scottish churches an air of quietness is adopted by the congregation – messages are passed one to another in whispers. Only the voice of the minister speaks naturally. Sometimes in these silent periods, the only sounds are the furtive unwrapping of sweet wrappers, or an occasional minty Pandrop dropping and bouncing noisily around the wooden floorboards.

Oh, how embarrassing.

Tut, tut, tut!

On this particular Sunday, Willie Bruce and the other members of the congregation took their places for the morning service.

He noted with satisfaction that a seat quite near to the choir was vacant. This was fine. The choirmaster could not fail to hear the quality of his voice from there.

When the minister announced hymn number 413, Willie glowed with anticipation; it was of course "Rock of ages cleft for me" – his favourite hymn.

He knew it well.

He would sing to the very best of his ability – loud and clear – he thought. This would be his best chance to obtain a place in the choir.

The organist, upon a deft upward flick from the choirmaster's baton, played the first bars of that well-known hymn, and the choir stood and turned to face the congregation.

The singing commenced:

> *Rock of Ages, cleft for me,*
> > *Let me hide myself in Thee;*
> *Let the water and the blood,*
> > *From Thy riven side which flowed,*
> *Be of sin the double cure,*
> > *Cleanse me from its guilt and power.*

It was then that things went awry... quite badly!

Let me explain. As you will perhaps know, these hymns can be sung to different tunes.

Unfortunately, Willie Bruce chose to sing just such a different tune. And with his dramatically powerful voice too. The man was so spiritually and emotionally involved with this, his favourite hymn, that he failed to notice that the choir and the congregation were doing their very best to weather the storm and keep to the path of the choirmaster's tune.

A different one.

The choirmaster's ruddy complexion turned sickly white, but bravely brandishing his baton, he endeavoured to whip up more volume from his now increasingly faltering and confused choristers.

As the choir faltered so too did the congregation.

Except for Willie Bruce.

Indeed, Willie's voice now rose to the very rafters, filling the church with its discordant sound.

The choirmaster's arms started to tire and, losing all hope, his baton slowly sank.

The minister, resting for a moment in his pulpit, got wearily to his feet, aware now that his spiritual ship was heading for the rocks in noisy clashing waves. Standing at the helm his voice commanded the tempest to cease and, with a steady hand, he steered his flock back to calmer waters where, apart from some unruly chuckles and sly winks passing from one to another, quiet once more reigned, and his sermon began.

Oh! But the sermon seemed to go on and on, feet were beginning to shuffle impatiently, their owners were growing anxious, all that was now in their minds was the thought of escape. How they were looking forward to the discussion of both Willie's and the choirmaster's performance.

Oh dear!

The choirmaster collared the minister after the service with an ultimatum, 'Get rid of Bruce or I'm finished!' he threatened.

The next morning the minister, glad that the fiasco of Sunday was behind him, chose to relax by taking a peaceful stroll down Shore Street, whereupon he spotted Willie Bruce loitering around.

Willie was also glad to have Sunday behind him, but only because he was now full of expectation that an invitation to join the choir was imminent.

And here was the minister himself, hailing him from across the street and saying, 'A word if you please, Mr. Bruce.'

Willie crossed jauntily over with a smile, thinking to himself – this is it, they heard me yesterday, I know I did well and here he is, the minister himself, to say so. Oh! The choir is the place for me.

'Good morning, Minister,' greeted Willie cheerily, 'and if it's about the singing, I'll be pleased to help in any way I can.'

His smile very quickly faded when the minister wondered if perhaps Mr. Bruce could moderate his singing, or, even better... *not sing at all*!

Having imparted these insensitive words the minister strolled on contentedly, leaving Willie Bruce shocked, humiliated, and very, very angry.

So angry indeed, that he was quite determined to find any sympathetic ear to tell all about it to.

Anger accompanied Willie Bruce as he stormed on down the street towards William the tailor's shop, near the Caledonian Hotel. Here he would unburden himself to the tailor, a person he knew well.

Of course, the tailor had heard all about the events that had taken place at the Church of Scotland the previous day, had his wife herself not been in the choir?

In the firing line – so to speak.

What a laugh!

The tailor listened to Willie Bruce's story with great sympathy, trying his best to keep a straight face.

At last Willie Bruce ended his angry rant by exclaiming loudly, 'I've a damn good mind to give up religion altogether and join the Frees.'

Adopting a very serious expression, my father – who happened to be the tailor – looked up from his work and murmured gravely:

'Surely not Willie. Anything, but *that*!'

The Nettle

....

In memory of my boyhood heroes:
William Mackenzie, my father;
Alexander Mackenzie, my uncle;
James Mackenzie, my cousin; and not
forgetting the Lochside men who gave them
such support all those years ago.

In 1926 Lord Stradbroke retired after years of service in Australia as Governor of Victoria and returned to England where he resumed living on the family's vast estate.

He was happy to be back in his native land and, being still in his middle years, was determined to enjoy his retirement to the full. While the estate in Suffolk was fine, his sojourn in Australia made him pine for something rather more adventurous.

In common with many aristocrats of the time,

he considered that the Highlands of Scotland was a fine place to go with its hunting, fishing and wild landscapes and he was able to secure the Inverlael estate at the south end of Loch Broom.

So that the new 'Lord' of Inverlael and his guests could voyage to the outer limits of Loch Broom for the fishing grounds and, of course, to visit the enchanting Summer Isles – it was found necessary to obtain a suitable yacht. After a search by Stradbroke's broker, the Nettle was purchased. She was a very fine vessel of forty feet in length and in perfect condition.

A further search by the broker found a suitable master for his Lordship's vessel – a Captain Auld. On paper, he seemed to fit all the requirements for the post and he was duly appointed and a crew was hired to deliver the vessel from Dumbarton to Loch Broom.

Captain Auld showed himself to be very pleased with the performance of his new command and all went well during the trip north. On arrival, the Nettle picked up the moorings laid for her in Loggie Bay, a quiet, sheltered location in the inner part of Loch Broom.

This would be her permanent anchorage.

Here, Captain Auld would reside aboard whilst awaiting orders from the owner, his duties being to look after the yacht and keep her in readiness at all reasonable times. This he did with a will as he loved his command.

It should be remembered perhaps, that despite his great ability in nautical matters, Captain Auld was still a young man. He was athletic and of good appearance and had become used to the more worldly excitements that were to be found in Glasgow and such places. and thus life at Loggie Bay seemed a bit dull to this young rake.

How quiet it was here.

In the few crofthouses scattered around the bay only Gaelic was spoken, a language the young man could not understand.

Mind you, Ullapool was not far distant, consequently, he took to rowing the two miles there with enthusiasm. Although, not quite so enthusiastically on the way back perhaps.

A small village Ullapool may have been, but there were shops enough for both his needs and the yacht's; moreover, the people in the village were friendly and spoke in his own tongue and to his immense relief, there were pubs aplenty, two of which actually hired bar-maids! Here he was warmly welcomed. He must come again, he told himself and so he did – unbeknownst to Lord Stradbroke – and with increasing frequency.

Trouble ahead?

Lord Stradbroke too found life at Inverlael and Loch Broom very much to his liking and with the added attraction of his "Jewel in the Crown" – the Nettle – lying at anchor and ready at a moment's notice to sail, he happily settled in for the long enjoyable years of retirement ahead.

In amongst his busy schedule of hunting and shooting and other estate commitments, Lord Stradbroke would on occasion find time to call on Captain Auld, issuing orders to take him and his guests out to open water where they would fish for skate and mackerel. and lounge on the polished teak decks to admire the beautiful coastal scenery scudding by. They watched as the sublime northern sun would set over the enchanted Summer Isles, glorying in the wild, beautiful isolation of this almost uninhabited world of sea and isles.

He couldn't have been happier.

You could perhaps forgive him for thinking that this grand spectacle had been created just for him.

And all this brought to him by his trusty Captain Auld; indeed Lord Stradbroke knew full well that he would not have been party to such magnificence without him.

When they saw the Nettle at sea, sailing by with her snowy sails wind-filled, the people of Ullapool would remark on her beauty:

There goes the Nettle.

Isn't she splendid?

And she was.

And life couldn't have been better.

If only the Nettle could have been put to more regular use things might have been different.

Captain Auld would have had more work and less play.

Oh, dear! Choppy water ahead.

On his Lordship's return from business in Suffolk one day, he was distressed to find himself at the receiving end of bad news. His Inverlael estate manager gleefully informed him of certain recent outrages conducted by his precious Captain Auld.

He regaled him with a veritable litany of events: being drunk and disorderly; fighting in the streets; and – oh, and worst of all – discharging a firearm to the great alarm of the congregation exiting the Established church – and on a Sunday morning too.

Oh, yes, the manager took great pleasure in

watching the blood burst into his Lordship's face which now boiled red with rage.

'Get Auld here right away!' his Lordship shouted.

You might have remarked that the estate manager did not much care for Captain Auld. You might also wonder why Captain Auld chose to go rampaging through the village after formerly so enjoying his visits there, drinking with his friends, as he did, and flirting with the girls?

It turns out that he was a man with a very short fuse and when he found out that his so-called "friends" were mocking him behind his back whenever he appeared dressed up in his yachting finery and calling him Captain Kettle...well... this he could not tolerate and action had to be taken.

Captain Kettle was a known rogue after all – albeit just a character in a book – who cared about nobody but himself.

A far cry from his own character was he not.

He had his reputation to consider.

He was a man of standing in the world, unlike these ruffian villagers.

Perhaps, you may think, the mirror has a habit of reflecting only that which you yourself want to see.

At any rate, this was apparently the cause of Auld's wild rampage.

The estate manager, in his turn, had his own score to settle. He desperately wanted to bring 'that damn *teuchter*' down a peg or two.

A case of there being only room enough for one cock to crow and with both men being thoroughly

Teuchter - a Lowland Scots word usually used to describe a Scottish Highlander. The term is usually used in fun, but can be derogatory, essentially describing someone seen to be uncouth and rural.   247

convinced that that cock should be himself.

By that particular Tuesday morning, Captain Auld had forgotten the frolics of the weekend and was busy tidying up the yacht in the hope that soon the vessel would put out to sea.

He was paying particular attention to the beautiful Gleniffer engine nestling down below in the immaculate engine room. Captain Auld was a good and diligent worker, he loved the Nettle and took pride in keeping all her brass and copper pipework burnished bright and so the engine was a joy to behold and a credit to him.

Suddenly he heard the thump-thump of a boat banging carelessly alongside the smooth hull.

He rushed up on deck to give the perpetrator a piece of his mind, only to be confronted with a Harris Tweed suit containing a weasel-faced man announcing in a rough voice, 'Get yourself up to the lodge! Himself is wanting a word!'

The tweed suit roughly thrust off from the gleaming ship's side and clumsily rowed the heavy dinghy away back to the shore of Loggie Bay.

Captain Auld, stunned at the cheek of the man, watched this oaf rowing leadenly to the beach, whereupon he almost capsized the little boat as he attempted to step gingerly from it to the shore in a failed attempt to stop from getting his gaiters wet. Once ashore he mounted his bicycle and disappeared up the path to the Lodge.

Auld was furious.

'Who the hell does he think he's speaking to?'. he fumed, 'Me! Me! The Captain of his Lordship's yacht! Bloody hillbilly!'

He had his dignity to maintain and he was

certainly not going to be at this man's beck and call, so he finished tidying up the Nettle before dressing in his shore-going uniform – appropriate attire for a meeting with Lord Stradbroke – and then launched the yacht's dinghy.

Stepping gracefully in, he rowed once around his command and observing everything to be neat and tidy he calmly headed across the narrows to where he would find the main road and where he would hopefully get a lift to Inverlael and the lodge.

Lord Stradbroke was still fuming away as he awaited the arrival of his ship's master. He knew, of course, where Auld had obtained the offending firearm – a Colt 45 – which had put the fear of God into the pious church folk, as he himself had rather foolishly left it aboard the yacht.

'I'll have to keep this quiet,' Stradbroke muttered to himself, 'I'll fire that mad dog with immediate effect.'

Anyway, he reasoned to himself, the yachting season is nearly over and I can do without a ship's master until next year.

Captain Auld, on arrival at Inverlael, was quickly marched into the presence of his boss. The staff at the lodge, their ears pressed against the door, listened with baited breath.

What would Himself do to the young Captain?

The stalkers let it be known that they would be more than pleased to take him out and use him for a bit of target practice.

The proceedings were brief and the staff scattered as the door opened and Captain Auld staggered out.

Poor man – he had learned that he was fired with immediate effect and he had been ordered to remove his effects from the Nettle '*this very day*'.

In total shock, he stumbled from the lordly presence into the company car which was instructed to deliver him to the narrows, from whence he could board the beloved yacht, of which he was no longer the master, and gather up his belongings and be gone.

The Captain, with sadness in his heart, rowed across the water to Loggie Bay and boarded the Nettle. He would have to remove himself from the yacht if he did not go then his Lordship's ruffians would certainly make sure that he did.

But was he himself not the proud seaman?

He promised himself that he would leave his beloved yacht in perfect trim. And this is what he fully intended to do. Visiting every compartment and cabin, his fingers touching tenderly here and there, he felt the voice of the vessel speaking and comforting him in turn... but, alas, these words were perhaps emanating from the spirits in the whisky bottle he had consumed on arriving back aboard.

The erstwhile Captain Auld finally went to the engine room and looked at the cooling pipework he had been so recently and lovingly polishing.

Had he finished that little job he had been in the middle of when he was interrupted by that conniving manager, he asked himself?

'Did I screw up the retaining nut?'

He had.

'Did I put back the seacock correctly?'

He had.

These cares, that he had taken so much to heart, now provoked a deep anger in him.

Why am I even bothered, he demanded of himself, they have not the least idea how much I love this ship and how much I do for her.

A thunderous rage was building in his head and, without further thought, he turned the seacock to the "Flood" position and left the engine room.

He quickly packed up his sea bag, boarded the dinghy and rowed back across the narrows before thumbing a lift from the butcher's van which was headed south.

He turned to look one final time at the Nettle as she swung easily at her moorings in answer to a slight breeze. Her brightly polished portholes glittered in the afternoon sun – glittering like the teardrops of a spurned lover, he couldn't help thinking.

For a moment Auld considered going back, to right the wrong he had committed, but at the van driver's urging to get a move on, Auld jumped in and fled the scene.

Never again to see his beloved Nettle.

Nobody noticed the yacht settling in the calm water of Loggie Bay. The slow and steady flow of water entering through the seacock brought about the sinking over a period of several hours. It was not until the following morning that the residents of the crofthouses noticed the emptiness of the bay.

Ah! She must be out sailing, they thought.

But then, what was that sticking up through the still water?

Was it a mast?

It was.

News of the tragedy quickly reached the Lodge and her owner was informed that his yacht was sitting on the bottom with only the tip of her mast showing.

I hope her Captain went down with the ship, damn

him, he thought, as he put in motion a claim for his loss with Lloyd's of London.

The surveyor was sent up at all speed, his Lordship being both customer and shareholder.

He quickly reported back, saying that in consideration of the isolated position of the sinking and there being no mechanical means of lifting the vessel in the region and, together with the excessive depth of the water in which she lay, that she should be declared a "constructive total loss" with the owner being paid out in full.

Head Office agreed and acting without delay the ownership of the Nettle was transferred from Lord Stradbroke to the insurers.

Not having any interest in the wreck, Lloyd's wanted to be rid of her as soon as possible, so the vessel was offered for sale in various newspapers:

"As she lay".

Salvage contractors were few and far between at that time and the nearest company which could do the job was at Scapa Flow where salvage work on the sunken German fleet was going on. For them, the Nettle was indeed not worth the bother.

Local people may have considered the salvage, but raising such a heavy yacht without the right equipment would have been nigh on impossible.

And so the Nettle was left to languish, for evermore, at the bottom of the loch.

THE MACKENZIE BROTHERS

In the village of Ullapool three businessmen could not stop thinking and talking about this fine yacht lying for all time on the seabed and, at a time of low water, onlookers were surprised to see these three unlikely persons viewing the site of the sinking.

There was William Mackenzie and his brother Alec, both of them tailors, and their cousin, James Mackenzie, a grocer.

How could they hope to salvage the Nettle?

Never in a thousand years!

Imagine it!

Oh, it was all a good laugh to these people.

The three men gazing down through water saw the dim wavering outline of this once fine vessel. They were careful and they knew their limitations; they knew too that they lacked the equipment necessary to raise such a large yacht.

Disconsolately, they left the scene.

But the challenge of an attempt, however impossible it would seem to be, could not be erased from their minds and so, despite their lack of experience and equipment, it was finally agreed that together they could afford to tender a very small sum in order to secure ownership of the wreck.

Would Lloyd's accept such a derisory amount?

They would.

Anxious to get this wreck off their books Lloyd's agreed to the offer and so the sunken Nettle was now under the title of the "Mackenzie Brothers", albeit under sixty feet of water.

William was perhaps forty-one years old at that time and Alec thirty-nine. Both were battle-hardened men who had survived the 1914-18 war in Flanders Field. They were used to having to get things done and done with very little. James, their cousin, was much younger, his contribution was his ability to drive and, most importantly, his access to transport. William had also worked as a rigger in the Naval

Dockyard at Invergordon and Alec had worked at the railway works in Glasgow – experience that would have been of help in this difficult endeavour.

Having gambled their precious funds in this unlikely project they had to take immediate steps to speedily recover their property from the seabed.

News of the changing ownership of Stradbroke's yacht was greeted with some surprise, especially when it was known that the new owners were the Mackenzie brothers – small time tailors in the village of Ullapool.

'What the heck will they do with that? And with sixty feet of water over her!' said a regular of the pub, addressing one equally knowledgeable patron.

Then, nodding to the barman to indicate that his glass was empty, he said, 'Put another dram in there, Sandy. Bloody fools! That's what I say!'

There is a satisfaction to be had in anticipating the failure of others and this man was eager to see it and, looking around at the grinning crowd, he was pleased to see that they shared in his hopes.

Oh, yes, in the Ullapool pubs, the whole episode was a joke. Indeed it was a happy continuum to the whole Nettle saga, and so they laughed uproariously at the brothers, along with the hilarious memories of "Captain Kettle" – now on the run from the law.

But let me tell you, on the Lochside and in Loggie and Letters, the story was received with interest and some respect. The people there remembered that both William and Alec were born at Loggie. Many of their relations still lived there, working the crofts on the Glebe, fishing the shoals of herring, netting the salmon and going away to crew the great yachts in the summer.

Oh! The brothers knew about boats, they said. They had built their own and knew about handling crafts of all sizes. The people from the Lochside also knew that men from Loggie never spent good money for fun. These men, were they not their own folk? They were, indeed! If the Mackenzie brothers needed help, then help would be given.

For the partners, the next few weeks were busy sourcing and collecting equipment for the salvage. The Lochsiders were quick to offer up potential buoyancy in the shape of old fishing boat hulls.

These boats, long since laid up, spoke of the decline of herring shoals in the loch and had been hauled up above the high-water line waiting for better times. Overturned, some had suffered the indignity of being put to use as sheds or henhouses.

Four of the most likely were selected, given a coat of tar and floated off in the hope that the shrunken planks would swell and become watertight.

Swell they did and became boats once more.

Tall larch trees were cut down at Leckmelm and trimmed and floated across to Loggie Bay. These would act as strongbacks in the lifting attempt to re-float the Nettle.

William wrote to his old mate – still working as chief rigger at Invergordon Naval dockyard – in the hope that heavy hemp rope could miraculously be found and be available – and it was.

James, with his van, was in charge of the collection and delivery of all usable gear to the site of the salvage attempt.

Try to picture the yacht – lying with a heavy list – her mast alone is penetrating the quiet surface of Loggie Bay. Tied to the masthead is the partners' workboat and seated therein are the three owners of this sunken vessel. The three men are discussing how they might rescue her from the seabed.

Plans are forming.

They are well aware that it is going to be difficult to place the lifting slings under the hull and they talk of the possibility of causing damage in so doing.

Holding onto the rigging all three feel a tremor running through the wire at the utterance of the word... damage.

They look questioningly at one another.

Is this the soul of the Nettle fearing the worst?

Superstitious nonsense.

Though indeed, the more the partners plan and work on the salvage, the more the yacht begins to insinuate herself into their affections.

That the Nettle had a soul was an idea that began to take hold.

With all the gear now gathered, their first job was to get the slings in place under the hull. A light chain was fished under her mooring, then under the bowsprit, before sawing its way aft under the forward part of the hull. The chain was coupled to the heavy hemp hawser and pulled through, bringing the lifting sling into place. The two ends were then temporarily made fast to the masthead.

In the same way, they positioned the after-lifting sling, taking great care not to damage the propeller and rudder.

So far, so good.

Progress.

The old fishing skiffs, now reasonably watertight, were floated over the wreck and lashed together, two on each side with the long, larch, strongbacks reaching over their gunwales. Everything was lashed tight using William's rigging expertise.

With the lowest tide of the year upon them, this was their chance. The lift had to commence and the great hemp slings would be put to the test and hauled taut over the strongbacks.

The question was, were the old skiffs buoyant enough to lift the Nettle, or would the lifting strain cause the wizened boats to break up?

Soon they would know.

The rising tide was already tightening the slings around the larch strongbacks.

Everything seemed to be going to plan, but as the tide steadily rose the buoyant skiffs were pulled lower and lower in the water and with no movement being felt in the Nettle the men started to become anxious.

Alec, with a sharpened axe in his hand, stood by, ready to chop the lifting slings should there not be enough buoyancy. Now with only inches of freeboard, the groaning skiffs were in danger of being overwhelmed.

In desperation, Alec cried out, 'I'm going to cut the ropes, William, or the whole bloody lot will be on the bottom.'

'Steady Alec, I feel her moving,' William's calming voice replied.

And true enough, the Nettle was rising, be it ever so gently, from the seabed.

Alec laid the axe down.

Now with a further three hours of tide to come, and with quiet satisfaction, the men prepared to shift the yacht into ever-shallower water.

The yacht was still secured to her mooring, so it

became necessary to uncouple her, and then, hauling steadily on the shore rope, the Nettle was slowly inched nearer to the land.

This was a slow haul over the next few days and tides, but finally she was grounded at high water on the steep shingle beach.

The men waited for the tide to recede before they climbed aboard the vessel and, armed with buckets, the Lochsiders started to bail out the ship. This they did with a will, bending eagerly to the work, but as much as they emptied she seemed to fill.

Was she damaged?

Did she sit on an old anchor on the seabed?

Ah, no – "strangely" the flood valve was open.

Once closed, she was pumped dry.

The soul of the Nettle descended happily from the masthead to more comfortable, if still pretty damp, accommodation in the hull.

'Never mind – these Mackenzie lads will soon fix that for me,' she whispered contentedly to herself.

The news that the Nettle was afloat soon reached Ullapool and in one bar a man could be heard to say:

'I knew those guys could do it! Remember me saying it, Sandy?'

Sandy shook his head in disbelief.

At Loggie Bay there was still much to do in preparing the Nettle for the move down the loch to Ullapool. The engine would have to be stripped, but that would have to wait until the Nettle was alongside the pier. All the lifting tackle was dismantled and the old fishing skiffs which had worked so well were returned to their retirement.

The hens at Letters were delighted to have their houses back again, cleaned and scoured as they were by the sea.

'Better than ever,' they clucked excitedly.

'And look, newly tarred and watertight too,' crowed the cockerel joyfully.

After a basic clean up the Nettle was ready to sail and this she did with the help of a kindly southerly breeze and a small amount of canvas set.

Word of her progress had reached the village and many locals had gathered on the pier to watch her arrival with the three jubilant Mackenzies aboard.

Surely nothing untoward could happen now - she was only a half a mile away from her destination.

The partners were aware that without the engine it might be difficult to go alongside the pier, but the weather was ideal with just a gentle breeze, even so, the sail was lowered well before the pier.

On approaching the inner corner of the pier a strong rope would be thrown up to the waiting crowd for someone to nimbly catch and drop its loop over the corner bollard and then, as the rope tightened, she would naturally swing into place alongside the sheltered inner side of the pier. That was the plan.

Alec Mackenzie threw the rope end ashore where at least six eager men stood ready to seize it.

Six men threw themselves at the rope and, in the melee, six men failed to grasp it.

William, standing at the helm, could not believe his eyes as he watched the rope slithering into the sea. There was nothing they could do as the Nettle glided on, before coming to an abrupt halt when the bowsprit hit the stonework of the pier and splintered along its entire length.

Poor Father.

He told me later that he could have died of shame.

Among the onlookers on the pier was Kenneth Campbell, a comrade in arms of both William and Alec. He was now a joiner – and funeral director (these being trades-in-arms in these parts) – and seeing their embarrassment, shouted down:

'Don't worry about that, William, worse things happened in France. I've a log in the yard that will make a new bowsprit.'

Cheered by his kind words they finally made the Nettle fast alongside.

Now at the pier, it was much easier to clean the yacht up and repair the small amount of damage done. True to his word Kenneth Campbell made and fitted a new bowsprit. Another old comrade, Alec Mackay, stripped the engine. A replacement magneto was all it took to have the gleaming Gleniffer purring like a contented cat once again.

When all was done Lloyd's of London were invited to reinsure the Nettle and, strange to say, the same surveyor who had declared the vessel a "constructive total loss" was instructed to survey her once more.

He came.

He saw.

He declared the yacht A1.

Well... on condition that the sea inlet to the flood valve be leaded over so that water would never enter there again.

What plan had the Mackenzies for the Nettle the locals wondered. She was a very prestigious yacht after all, would they keep her and live like lords aboard?

No.

They could not afford such a fine ship.

And so the Nettle was sailed back to McAlister's yard at Dumbarton from whence she came, and from where she quickly found a new master who had the time to appreciate her and, more importantly, the means.

And appreciated she was.

She sailed the seas for many a long day, I believe, and to the entire satisfaction of her soul who remembered, with much gratitude and fondness, her rescuers – the Mackenzie brothers.

Herring for Christmas

....

At last Hendrick, the skipper of the Pandora, was satisfied; the boat was fully laden with silver herring, which had been carefully salted and – just as carefully – stowed below in wooden barrels, which had been wedged in tight in case of heavy weather on the long voyage around the north coast to Holland and her home port – Goedereede.

He was keen to be off the island of Tanera Mòr, and he cast his eye anxiously over the full hold and the deck, which had been loaded with ten more barrels, now lashed to the rails.

The skipper felt lucky to have secured such a catch, and he had gladly accepted these additional barrels knowing how much of a delicacy they were to the Dutch peoples.

Standing alongside the manager of the curing station Hendrick smiled, and together they watched as the newly-recruited, young Russian seaman – Kolya – checked the cargo.

A good hand, the skipper thought with pleasure.

'Are you sure about the weather? Should you not delay?' asked the manager.

The sky was indeed darkening, and a wind was picking up.

'No, no,' he replied, 'it's a favourable breeze.'

And shaking hands in farewell they cast off and set a course for Cape Wrath, hopeful that they would catch that swift current which would help carry Pandora and her treasure of silver around the wild, northern coast.

With the wind astern, the sails were set and full, and she was hurtling along at good speed – though the gusts were growing ever stronger.

Hendrick was at the wheel and Kolya standing alongside.

As the weather worsened, the skipper's mind was at work; he had a responsibility to the boat, as well as to this young seaman, but he also had to reach Goedereede in time for the Christmas market – it had been a hard year and his wife and children were counting on him. For the moment though everything was in order, and although the Pandora was labouring through the swell with the extra weight on her deck pushing her head down, she was managing.

'Press on, Pandora,' he murmured.

Kolya looked unperturbed.

'Good man, Kolya,' said the skipper smiling at the lad, who flashed him a grin in reply.

As the south-westerly wind increased Hendrick ordered that the hard-pressed sails be eased. Kolya left the skipper at the wheel, and labouring unsteadily across the rolling deck and fighting against the wind, he reduced the sail – instantly the ship's head lifted.

Now, while this is a tale of men and fish, it is also a tale of a boat.

Oh! That's better!' sighed Pandora as she pitched and rolled in the mighty waves. Her master could be a hard man sometimes, but he did care for her.

Knowing that he would never endanger her she was content to push on.

It is also a tale of the elements who live alongside her, as without the wind and the sea there would be no boats, and this simple fact filled the mighty Wind and the rollicking Sea with a sense of power and self-importance, and they had become very contemptuous of these insignificant little beings going who knows where.

So it was with some irritation that they noticed the Pandora out when they had so evidently sent a signal for all afloat to scurry home for shelter and leave them to themselves.

'Wind, my friend, Hey! Wind! Do you see that darned fishing smack lolling about on me? It's a total lack of respect, is it not? Don't you agree?'

'I do, I DO!' roared Wind.

They were a mischievous pair and had little concern for others, so between themselves they decided to have some fun.

Wind readied himself to perform a little squall, he loved the sound of his own voice, so there would be a howling and a hoo-ing too; and Sea donned her best sea-feathers – she swathed herself in white horses, spindrift, and enormous black, silken waves.

'Ha! We'll teach them!' they shouted in unison

and unleashed their theatre of mischief.

Poor Pandora was knocked sideways with this new onslaught; she could hear the thud of the barrels as they shifted around deep within her, and the straining and groaning of the heavy rope lashings.

"I do hope they hold,' she moaned.

If they didn't? Well, with the barrels free they would roll as one enormous mass to the side – she would capsize – it would be over for them all.

'Kolya!' Hendrick was shouting through the wailing tempest.

'Kolyaaah! Go forward and check the cargo!'

Kolya disappeared into the darkness of the rain and storm. The horizon was no more – the sky and sea had become one. The skipper glimpsed the young Russian through this fractured scene clinging desperately to the deck rail. Pandora was pitching and rolling as never before, but he saw with relief that somehow Kolya had scrambled on forward.

Wind, watching the crab-like motions of the young man from above, whipped himself around and blew with all his might onto the starboard beam, throwing poor Pandora over to port and her beam-ends. Her sails were now mere strips of flapping, screaming canvas, her yards banged like claps of thunder. Pandora bravely hove-to and righted herself, but then with a great wave Sea rose on up and over her stern – Kolya was caught up in the blackness of her net and pulled overboard. In the confusion Pandora ran right over him, she felt his body sweep under her rusty keel from bow to stern, and then he was gone. Spat out into the dark elements.

Gone...

Hendrick looked on in horror, powerless before

these forces of nature. He shouted curses upon them.

Wind, still excited by his little drama crowed down to Sea, 'That'll teach 'em, eh!'

Sea, perhaps more conscious of the role that she had played in Kolya's demise, heard his words and felt a sorrow. They had not wished to do any real harm, and yet they had taken the life of an innocent man.

She must right this wrong.

She called upon her currents and in the deeps they found his lifeless body. She wrapped him in her warm Gulf Stream and drew him up to the surface in the lee of an island. Thereupon, she called to Wind and Moon to help. As the dawn rose Moon raised a tide, and a now repentant Wind blew him gently high above the water line.

Blustering and crying out – 'I'm sorry!' – he puffed his warm breath into Kolya's drowned lungs.

Kolya coughed and spluttered.

Now, in this sheltered place there was a little cottage, and within this little cottage lived the MacLean family.

'What a wild night!' said Andrew to his wife as he stumbled out of bed to check if everything was still in place. He drew the curtains for his habitual look over the shoreline.

'What is that?' he shouted in alarm.

He called for his daughter, Millie.

'Get up, Millie, there's a body ashore.'

Father and daughter rushed down to the beach.

'Oh, dear Lord, he's dead!' said Andrew.

Kolya looked like a corpse indeed. His body was a bruised purple pulp. Millie knelt down beside him and, putting her cheek to his mouth, she felt the coolness of but the slightest of breaths.

They dragged him back to the warmth of their little house in an old sailcloth, and there he was slowly brought back to the land of the living.

Millie took charge of this young fellow and so it was to her lovely face that he awoke.

'Where am I?' he cried out in astonishment.

The family smiled.

'He'll live!' they chorused happily.

Some days later a Dutch ship – the Louisa – anchored in the bay to replenish her fresh water and to make some repairs following the terrible storm.

The father looked over to Millie and Kolya; he could see a look of tenderness – and was that love? – in his daughter's eyes as she busied herself with her patient – a look that was mirrored in the lad's eyes.

'Row out to the ship, daughter, and ask the Captain if he might take Kolya home with him. He needs more help than we can give.'

As she rowed Millie bowed her head and spilled some salty tears into the sea.

Sea heard her weeping and felt the pain that she had caused to this young lassie too. Their little game had gone so amiss.

The Captain willingly took Kolya onboard and assured the family that he would one day return and, hopefully, the young Russian might be aboard. His kind words were meant to help, but as the girl watched sadly from the shore, the ship spread her sails and like a huge white bird she winged herself away to a far-off land carrying with it Millie's hopes and dreams.

Now, that would be a sad end for the story would it not?

Wind, looking down on this forlorn little figure, shouted to his friend Sea, 'We have to make amends! I am going to fill the sails of this ship and send her swiftly on!'

'And I will hold back my waves!' called Sea.

'Indeed, I will send out my most powerful currents to push her along!'

The Louisa's Captain had never before sailed in such favourable circumstances, and he was amazed to find himself pulling into Goedereede in record time. After docking the crew had merrily set to – backs bent – and were swinging the heavy baskets of fish ashore when they noticed the Pandora slinking in astern of them.

Hendrick, looking grey and ashen, threw a line over to a couple of men standing on the pier and watched as one of them hobbled to catch it.

He had to rub his eyes – was this grinning youth not the very same one that he had given up for dead?

Rushing down to his cabin he dug out the Christmas tree that, in his grief, he had planned on throwing into the sea, and with a new found agility he scrambled up the rigging and lashed the 'tree of promise' to the masthead.

'Oh, Kolya, you are the best Christmas present a man could hope to receive!' Hendrick cried hugging him tight. The Russian groaned in pain at this exuberant show of affection, but a broad smile was stretched over his handsome face.

Wind and Sea watched this reunion with pleasure.

They knew that the silver treasure in Pandora's hold was just in time for the Christmas market and would make a good price – Hendrick and his family would be content, and they happily observed the skipper as he draped his arm across the young man's shoulders and hugged him once more.

Their terrible wrong had at last been righted.

And now we see Kolya's eyes gazing north, and as the first soft flakes of snow fall like feathers, we know where he will be next Christmas.

ABOUT THE AUTHOR

Macnab 'Nabbie' Mackenzie was born in Ullapool in 1931. As a child he loved writing stories, but becoming an author was not even a consideration for a young Highland man in those days.

However, he also loved building and tinkering with engines and boats, and so he trained as an apprentice engineer at Wm. Denny's in Dumbarton.

On completion of his apprenticeship he worked as an engineer on ships sailing to South America, the Falklands, South Georgia, the Antarctic, and around the Cape to Australia, New Zealand, Hong Kong, Malaya (as it was then known), Singapore, and the many coastal countries in between.

In 1956 he met Marjorie, a young nurse, in Southampton and they married the following year and returned to Ullapool. Here he turned his hand to working in a quarry and building roads; at the same time the young couple built and opened a petrol station and garage.

With a growing family to feed and clothe, he left to work at Dounreay nuclear power station on the north coast of Scotland, while Marjorie ran the petrol station and looked after the children.

They invested in a boat, the 'Summer Queen', and worked for many years taking visitors to Tanera Mòr and the Summer Isles; their house became a B&B.

In the 1970's they bought work-boats, running supplies and crew to the Russian and Eastern European factory ships anchored around Ullapool, and when the Russians left, and money got tight once more, Nabbie worked for a time on the fishing boats whilst slowly building up his business. Before he retired Mackenzie Marine boats were on charter all around the UK.

Nabbie has always been a storyteller, and his yarns revolve around his life and memories – sea, boats, family, the village, and people he has known – and in recent years he has been writing them down and sending them to the local paper - the Ullapool News.

The family gathered his stories together for this book in order to share his yarns more widely, but also to raise money for Great Ormond Street Hospital Charity.

It was there, in 1972, that Marjorie and Nabbie's son, Simon, underwent a pioneering heart operation.

He was only two years old.

Although Simon passed away in 2014, the doctors and nurses of Great Ormond Street Hospital had given him the gift of many more years of life, for which the family are eternally grateful.

Through the sale of Nabbie's Yarns we hope to keep on returning that gift, therefore all proceeds from the sale of this book go to Great Ormond Street Hospital Charity in memory of Simon Macnab Mackenzie and Marjorie Mackenzie

info@nabbiesyarns.co.uk

www.nabbiesyarns.co.uk

twitter.com/NabbieY (old photos of Ullapool and family)

ACKNOWLEDGEMENTS

Inquiring with Chris Brotherston as to whether her publishing my stories in our august local paper ~ the Ullapool News ~ had dramatically decreased their sales, I was heartened to hear her response:

'Not *so* far,' said she.

I breathed a sigh of relief.

So, many thanks to the whole team at the Ullapool News, Chris of course, and Jo Scott, Barbara Jackson, Sheila Didcock, Jimmy Lavelle, Celia Mackenzie, Alexander Mackenzie, Audrey Maclennan, Catriona Martin, Kenneth Morrison, Heather Wallace and Ray Forsyth.

And thanks also to Don Shaw – who worked at the Ullapool Bookshop for many years – for his advice and for writing a very nice synopsis. And to Kath Bell for suggesting that a map might be a useful guide.

And finally, thank you to the dear readers of the Ullapool News for all the kind words, and the encouragement that you have given me over the years.

27507482R00174

Printed in Poland
by Amazon Fulfillment
Poland Sp. z o.o., Wrocław